THE SAGA OF
DARREN SHAN
TUNNELS OF BLOOD

VOLUME
3

Story: Darren Shan
Manga: Takahiro Arai

A SUMMARY OF CIRQUE DU FREAK:

DARREN SHAN IS TURNED INTO A HALF-VAMPIRE IN ORDER TO SAVE HIS BEST FRIEND'S LIFE. HIS PEACEFUL LIFE GONE, DARREN STARTS ANEW WITH HIS MASTER, MR. CREPSLEY, AS A MEMBER OF THE CIRQUE DU FREAK. THOUGH HE MAKES TWO NEW FRIENDS THERE IN EVRA VON, THE SNAKE-BOY, AND SAM GREST, HIS HAPPY NEW ARRANGEMENT IS SHATTERED WHEN THE CIRQUE'S CHAINED WOLF-MAN ESCAPES AND KILLS SAM. BURDENED WITH A TERRIBLE SADNESS, DARREN RETREATS INTO THE DARKNESS AGAIN...

TUNNELS OF BLOOD
CONTENTS

EVRA AND I ARE ON A VISIT TO A RUN-DOWN WAREHOUSE IN A LITTLE TOWN, FAR FROM WHERE WE MET SAM.

IT'S BEEN OVER A YEAR SINCE SAM'S DEATH.

CHAPTER 15:
GAVNER PURL

I'VE LEARNED HOW TO SURVIVE WITH HUMAN BLOOD.

AFTER I DRANK SAM'S BLOOD, I MADE THE DECISION TO LIVE THE VAMPIRE WAY.

THIS IS LEFTY.

PON PON (PAT)

THANKS, LEFTY.

I STILL LOOK THE SAME, BUT ON THE INSIDE, MY BODY IS STRONGER AND MY SENSES ARE SHARPER.

DOSA (FLOP)

LET'S EAT, THEN.

I GOTCHA.

HE'S DIFFERENT FROM THE OTHERS. HE HELPED US BURY SAM.

BRRR! COLD!

LUCKY GUY. HE DOESN'T HAVE TO FORAGE FOR HIS FOOD.

WE CALL HIM "LEFTY" BECAUSE THE LIMP ON HIS LEFT LEG DISTINGUISHES HIM FROM THE OTHER LITTLE PEOPLE.

HOW ABOUT MADAM OCTA?

ARE THE PREPARATIONS MADE FOR OUR NEXT PERFORMANCE?

I GET ALONG WITH MR. CREPSLEY NOW. HE'S LIKE MY TEACHER IN LIFE.

I DON'T HATE HIM LIKE I DID WHEN HE FIRST TURNED ME INTO A HALF-VAMPIRE.

NU (LOOM)

OF COURSE. HOW LONG HAVE I BEEN DOING THIS?

SFX: PORI (MUNCH)

HA-HA, OF COURSE.

ONE MOVE AND YOU'RE DEAD, LARTEN CREPSLEY!

FREEZE!

GIRA (SHING)

KLED ONS

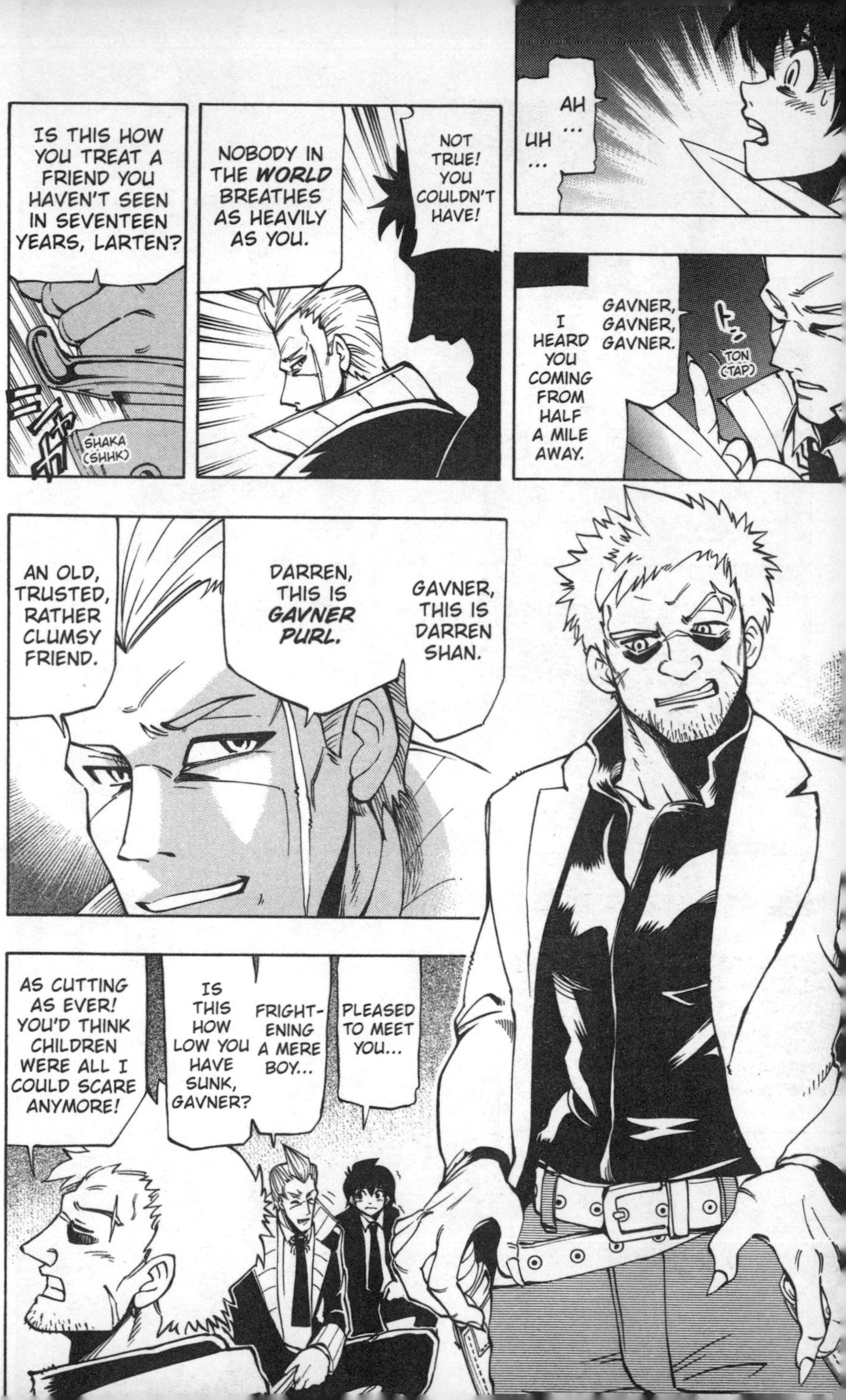
AH ... UH ...
GAVNER, GAVNER, GAVNER.
I HEARD YOU COMING FROM HALF A MILE AWAY.
TON (TAP)
NOT TRUE! YOU COULDN'T HAVE!
NOBODY IN THE WORLD BREATHES AS HEAVILY AS YOU.
IS THIS HOW YOU TREAT A FRIEND YOU HAVEN'T SEEN IN SEVENTEEN YEARS, LARTEN?
SHAKA (SHHK)
GAVNER, THIS IS DARREN SHAN.
DARREN, THIS IS GAVNER PURL.
AN OLD, TRUSTED, RATHER CLUMSY FRIEND.
PLEASED TO MEET YOU...
FRIGHT-ENING A MERE BOY...
IS THIS HOW LOW YOU HAVE SUNK, GAVNER?
AS CUTTING AS EVER! YOU'D THINK CHILDREN WERE ALL I COULD SCARE ANYMORE!

WE KEEP AN EYE ON SCOUNDRELS LIKE THESE!

DON (SHOVE)

WHAT IS A VAMPIRE GENERAL?

YOU MIGHT BE SURPRISED TO LEARN THAT GAVNER IS A VAMPIRE GENERAL.

THE VAMPIRE GENERALS MONITOR THE BEHAVIOUR OF THE VAMPIRE CLAN.

JUDGE? HOW?

...THEY HAVE THE AUTHORITY TO JUDGE THE GUILTY.

IF THEY FIND ANY OF US KILLING INNOCENTS OR USING OUR POWERS FOR EVIL...

CHIRA (GLANCE)

PARDON ME A MOMENT, DARREN...

I'M MORE LIKE A VILLAGE POLICEMAN THAN A SOLDIER...

OH, IT'S NOT SO SERIOUS AS ALL THAT.

SU (SHH)

KILL?!

THEY CAN KILL THE OFFENDING VAMPIRE.

I KNEW NOTHING OF THE KIND! HE'S NOTHING BUT A BOY! WHY?!

OF COURSE NOT!

BUT SURELY YOU KNEW. IS THAT NOT WHY YOU CAME TO SEE ME?

THIS BOY'S A VAMPIRE!

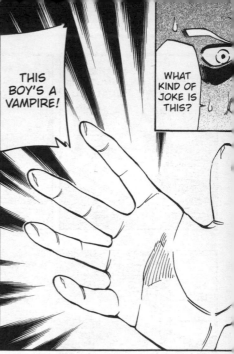

WHAT KIND OF JOKE IS THIS?

WHY I DID IT IS A LONG STORY...

YOU CAN JUDGE MY ACTIONS AND PASS VERDICT, GAVNER.

NOW I WILL NOT NEED TO TAKE HIM TO THE VAMPIRE COUNCIL.

SFX: DOSA (THUMP)

W-WHAT DO YOU MEAN ...?

I'VE COME ON A DIFFERENT MATTER! IT'S A PERSONAL ISSUE ...

ME? JUDGE YOU?

NO THANKS! I'LL LEAVE YOU TO THE COUNCIL!

GAVNER AND I HAVE MATTERS TO DISCUSS.

DARREN, I MUST ASK THAT YOU GIVE US PRIVACY.

I HAVE NO OBJECTIONS TO SPEAKING IN FRONT OF DARREN.

BUT...

SFX: KOKU (NOD)

HUH? BUT...

PLEASE FIND MR. TALL AND INFORM HIM I SHALL BE UNABLE TO PERFORM TONIGHT.

YOU'RE FINALLY GETTING A CHANCE TO DO THE ACT BY YOURSELF!

THAT'S GREAT, DARREN!

ONLY JOKING!

STOP THIS, GAVNER!

I'LL TELL YOU ALL ABOUT IT, AS SOON AS LARTEN'S BACK IS TURNED.

DON'T WORRY, DARREN!

THEY DON'T HAVE TO TREAT ME LIKE A KID...

SFX: PAN (CLAP)

W-WHAT IS IT, TRUSKA?!

TATA (TEK TEK)

MAYBE YOU'RE RIGHT...

YOUR OUTFIT'S NOT FLASHY ENOUGH FOR A ONE-MAN PERFORMANCE, THOUGH.

HEY, LOOKING GOOD! IT'S DARREN THE PIRATE!

WOW!!

THANKS, TRUSKA.

I'LL PUT ON A GREAT SHOW!

NIKO (GRIN)

HEY,
DARREN!

HEH
HEH
...

I DID PRETTY
WELL WITHOUT
MR. CREPSLEY
TOO!

MAN,
THAT
WAS
FUN!

WHAT DID YOU MEAN ABOUT MR. CREPSLEY BEING JUDGED?

WILL YOU TAKE A WALK WITH ME?

I'VE GOT TO BE LEAVING SOON.

SUTA (TUMP)

SURE...

THAT'S WHY WE HAVE A RULE THAT CHILDREN SHOULD NEVER BE BLOODED.

CHILDREN DON'T UNDER-STAND THE NATURE OF THE RISKS THEY'RE TAKING.

LARTEN MADE A MISTAKE. HE SHOULD NOT HAVE BLOODED YOU.

LARTEN IS WIDELY RE-SPECTED, YOU SEE.

I DOUBT IT.

WILL... WILL HE BE KILLED?

LARTEN WILL HAVE TO ACCOUNT FOR HIS ERROR IN BLOODING YOU.

IN THE CASE OF CHILDREN, THE SHOCK OF THE CHANGES IS DIFFICULT TO WITH-STAND...

MR. CREPSLEY WAS NEARLY A GREAT LEADER?

THAT'S WHAT WE CALL OUR LEADERS. THERE ARE VERY FEW OF THEM, AND ONLY THE NOBLEST AND MOST RESPECTED VAMPIRES ARE ELECTED!

PRINCE?

HE WAS ON THE VERGE OF BEING VOTED A VAMPIRE PRINCE!

HE USED TO BE A VAMPIRE GENERAL!

WHY WOULD HE DO THAT?

AND THEN HE LEFT US AND DISAPPEARED, ALL ON HIS OWN.

BUT HE STEPPED DOWN BEFORE IT COULD HAPPEN.

BEST NOT TO ASK.

SORRY, DARREN. LARTEN'LL SCALP ME ALIVE IF I TELL YOU MORE.

MAYBE HE JUST GOT TIRED OF THE FIGHTING AND KILLING ...

NOBODY KNOWS. LARTEN NEVER GAVE MUCH AWAY.

YOU'RE LEAVING? I WANTED TO HEAR MORE.

WELL, I SHOULD BE OFF ...

TRUST HIM, DARREN, AND YOU WON'T GO WRONG.

LISTEN, DARREN.

NO MATTER WHAT HAPPENS, STICK WITH LARTEN.

STICK WITH LARTEN AND LEARN EVERYTHING HE TEACHES YOU.

THIS CAN BE A DANGEROUS WORLD FOR VAMPIRES.

YOU COULDN'T HOPE FOR A BETTER TEACHER.

HE'S A GOOD VAMPIRE, ONE OF THE BEST.

HOW OLD *IS* HE?

IT'S THE ONLY WAY YOU'LL LIVE AS LONG AS HE HAS.

SFX: GUSHI GUSHI (RUMPLE)

PON (PAT)

PICTURE TRYING TO BLOW OUT THE CANDLES ON *THAT* CAKE!!

HOO (COOH)

I'VE GOT MY SIGHTS SET ON A THOUSAND, THOUGH!

I'M A WHIPPERSNAPPER, BARELY PAST THE HUNDRED MARK!

THAT OLD?!

I'M NOT SURE. I THINK ABOUT 180, MAYBE 200.

WAIT! WHAT DO YOU MEAN...

LARTEN WILL BE ON THE MOVE SOON, HIMSELF.

UNTIL NEXT TIME, GAVNER PURL.

SO LONG, DARREN SHAN.

HE SAID *YOU* MIGHT BE LEAVING TOO...

YES...

GACHA (CLICK)

GAVNER'S GONE.

KON (TAP)

KON

WHAT ELSE DID HE SAY?

...

GIRO (GLARE)

M-ME TOO?!

YOU WILL NEED TO PACK AS WELL.

AS IT HAPPENS, I WILL HAVE TO LEAVE THE CIRQUE FOR A WHILE.

N-NOTHING ...

I DON'T WANT TO LEAVE MY FRIENDS ...

BUT I LIKE IT HERE.

...BUT I THINK I MUST. I MAY HAVE NEED OF YOU.

I WOULD PREFER NOT TO TAKE YOU WITH ME...

THIS IS A MEANS OF COVER, NOT OUR HOME.

REMEMBER: WE ARE VAMPIRES, NOT CIRCUS PERFORMERS.

I WILL GO AND CLEAR IT WITH MR. TALL.

BUT IT'S TOO SUDDEN!

I TRUST YOU ARE AGREEABLE WITH THAT?

VERY WELL... WE SHALL BRING ALONG EVRA TOO.

HUH? BUT...

CONVINCE HIM TO COME.

YOU WILL HAVE TO EXPLAIN THIS TO EVRA.

...AND THAT'S THE PLAN.

HMMM ...

WHAT DO YOU SAY? ARE YOU COMING?

REALLY ?!

I'M NOT SURE HOW LONG WE'LL BE AWAY FROM THE CIRQUE, THOUGH...

YEAH! I'M WITH YOU ALL THE WAY!

YOU BET!

GOTSUN (BUMP)

I'VE NEVER BEEN SWIMMING OR TO THE CINEMA!

AN EXTENDED VACATION, THEN!

THANKS, EVRA!

I'M SURE SAM WILL LOVE IT TOO!

ZAWA

ZAWA (HUSTLE)

BE STRONG...

NOT AT ALL. DO NOT WORRY ABOUT US.

I AM SORRY THIS COMES SO SUDDENLY, HIBERNIUS.

KOKU (NOD)

YEAH. I LIKE THEM, AND MY OLD CLOTHES ARE FALLING APART.

ARE YOU REALLY GONNA GO IN THOSE, DARREN?

GOODBYE, LEFTY.

UH, YEAH...

YIKES!

TAKE GOOD CARE OF MADAM OCTA, HANS. MAKE SURE SHE DOESN'T BITE YOU.

MY SNAKE WILL BE HIBERNATING. MAKE SURE TO CHECK ON IT FROM TIME TO TIME!

THERE ARE NO LAWS AGAINST VAMPIRES USING PUBLIC TRANSPORTATION.

I SUPPOSE NOT...

BUSES AND TRAINS.

I WILL NOT BE FLITTING.

WILL YOU BE ABLE TO CARRY BOTH OF US WHEN YOU FLIT?

THEN HOW ARE WE GOING TO TRAVEL?

AND SO WE SAID OUR FAREWELLS TO THE CIRQUE DU FREAK AND HEADED OUT FOR A FAR-OFF CITY...

...WITHOUT ANY IDEA OF THE EVIL TWIST OF DESTINY THAT AWAITED US THERE...

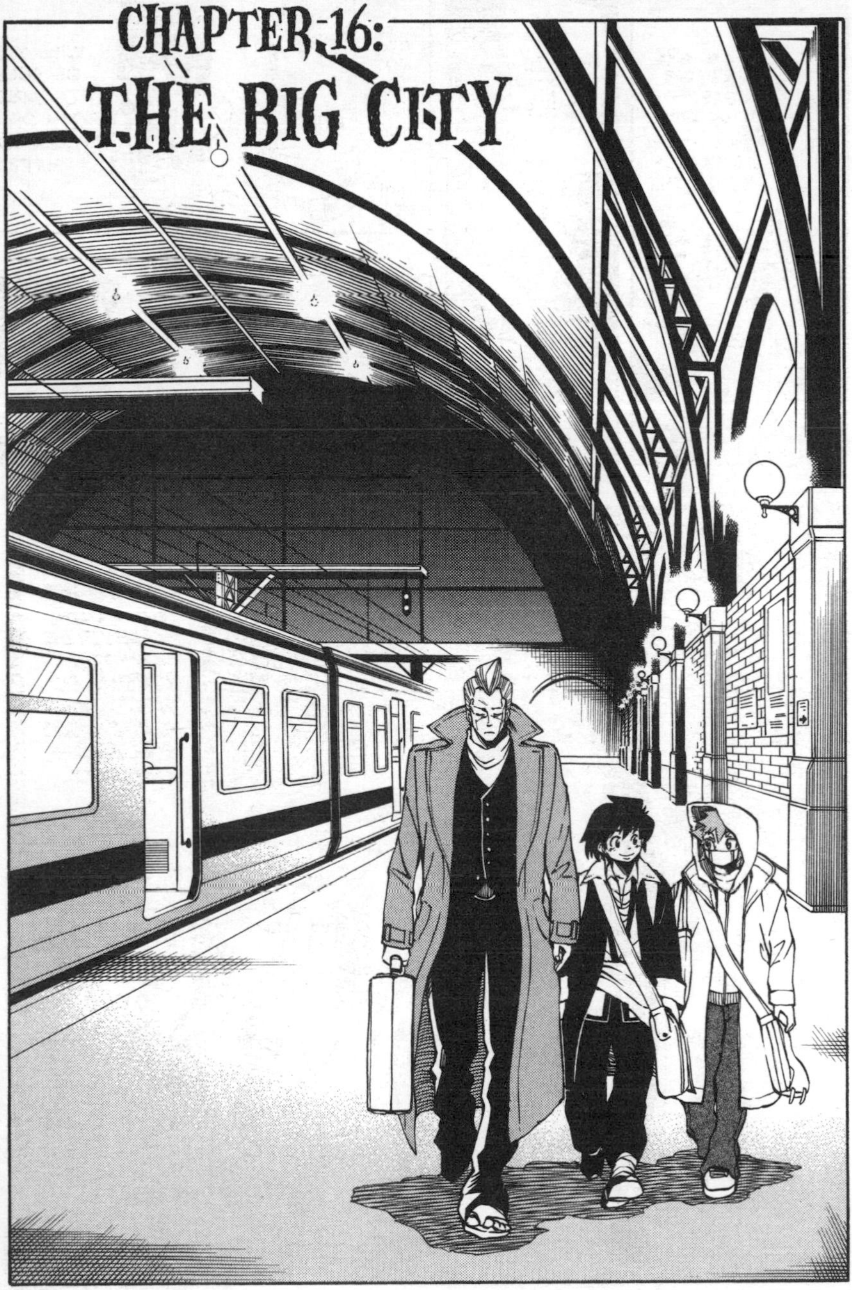
CHAPTER 16:
THE BIG CITY

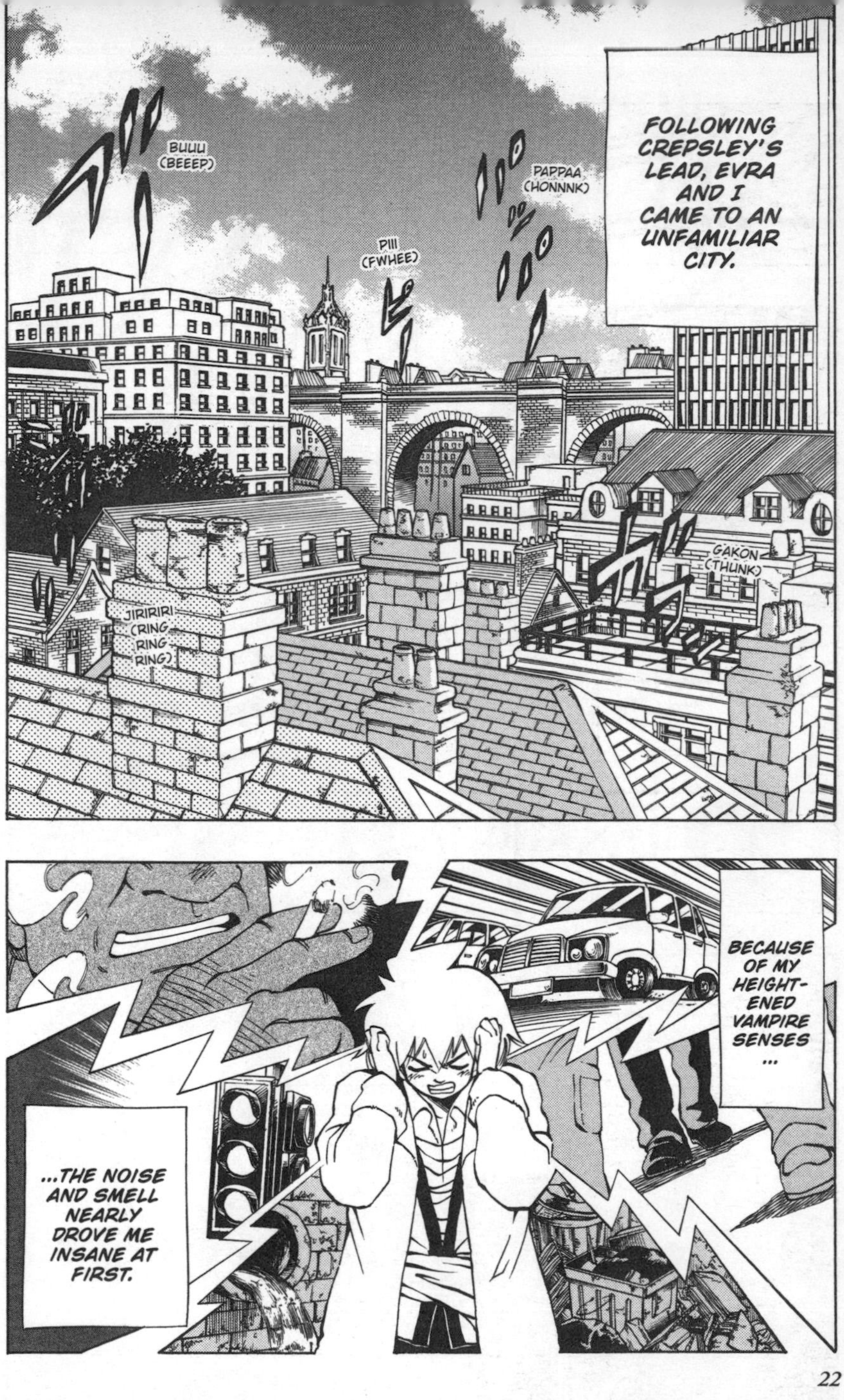
FOLLOWING CREPSLEY'S LEAD, EVRA AND I CAME TO AN UNFAMILIAR CITY.
BUUU (BEEEP)
PAPPAA (HONNNK)
PIII (FWHEE)
GAKON (THUNK)
JIRIRIRI (RING RING RING)
BECAUSE OF MY HEIGHTENED VAMPIRE SENSES ...
...THE NOISE AND SMELL NEARLY DROVE ME INSANE AT FIRST.

SHA
(WHISK)

...AND I FINALLY STARTED ENJOYING LIFE WITH EVRA.

BY THE END OF THE FIRST WEEK, I'D GOT USED TO IT, THOUGH...

MORNING, EVRA.

YAWWWN!

AT NIGHT WE'D STUFF OUR FACES, WATCH TV, AND PLAY VIDEO GAMES!

OOOH!

THEN WE'D COVER UP EVRA'S SCALES AND EXPLORE THE TOWN.

WE'D GET UP LATE AND EAT A BIG BREAK-FAST.

NEMU NEMU (YAWWND)

IN FACT, EVEN NORMAL PEOPLE DIDN'T HAVE IT THIS GOOD—THEY HAD TO GO TO WORK OR SCHOOL DURING THE DAY.

I NEVER REALIZED TV COULD BE SO ADDICTIVE!

AFTER A YEAR WITH THE CIRQUE DU FREAK, IT WAS A THRILL TO LIVE LIKE A NORMAL HUMAN AGAIN.

GACHA (CLICK)

HOW DO THEY DO IT?

THIS BAND IS THE GREAT-EST!

GYUIIIN (DAHHH)

WE WERE IN HEAVEN!

...AND HE'D COME HOME TIRED IN THE MORN-ING.

クヮ

BATAN (THUMP)

MR. CREPSLEY WENT OFF AT NIGHT WITHOUT TELLING US WHERE...

THAT'S JUST HOW MUCH FUN THINGS WERE!

HE HAD NEVER ACTED THIS SECRETIVELY BEFORE, BUT IT DIDN'T BOTHER ME MUCH.

HE WOULD NOT ANSWER A SINGLE QUESTION ABOUT WHERE HE WENT.

MORE WHAT?

COME ON, EVRA, IT'S *CHRISTMAS!* YOU SHOULD BE MORE...

YEAH.

SUTA (TROMP)

SUTA

IT'S ALREADY DECEMBER. CHRISTMAS IS COMING SOON, THEN.

I SEE IT.

LOOK, EVRA, A CHRISTMAS TREE!

YOU DON'T UNDERSTAND. CHRISTMAS IS MORE ABOUT SPENDING TIME WITH YOUR FAMILY AND SPREADING GOODWILL.

...AND PAY A LOT OF MONEY TO EXCHANGE PRESENTS. WHAT'S THE BIG DEAL?

YOU CUT DOWN TREES, KILL A LOT OF TURKEYS...

...BUT EVRA DOESN'T.

OF COURSE. I'VE GOT NOTHING BUT GOOD MEMORIES OF MY FAMILY...

OH.

YEAH...BUT WHAT DO I KNOW ABOUT FAMILY?

HYU (ZIP)

HEADS UP, DARREN!

YOU'RE GONNA GET IT!

HEH-HEH! HERE'S ANOTHER ONE!

TA (TEK)

BAFU (BOP)

WATCH OUT, THEN!

HA HA HA!

AHA HA HA!

DON'T THROW *TOO* HARD, DARREN!

NO, IT'LL BE QUICK.

WHERE YA GOIN', DARREN?

WANT ME TO COME?

IT SOFTENS THE NOISES AND SMELLS OF THE CITY.

I LOVE THE SNOW...

I'LL BE BACK BEFORE MR. CREPSLEY WAKES UP.

THE SNOW'S HEAVY OUTSIDE.

26

WITH THIS MUCH, I CAN BUY JUST ABOUT ANYTHING!

I'VE GOT MONEY FROM CREPSLEY.

I WANT TO MAKE THIS CHRISTMAS SO MUCH FUN...

NOT BEING ABLE TO ENJOY CHRISTMAS IS LIKE MISSING OUT ON A BIG PART OF LIFE.

...EVRA CAN'T HELP BUT FALL IN LOVE WITH IT!

AHOY, CAP'N!

I WONDER WHAT HE'D LIKE...

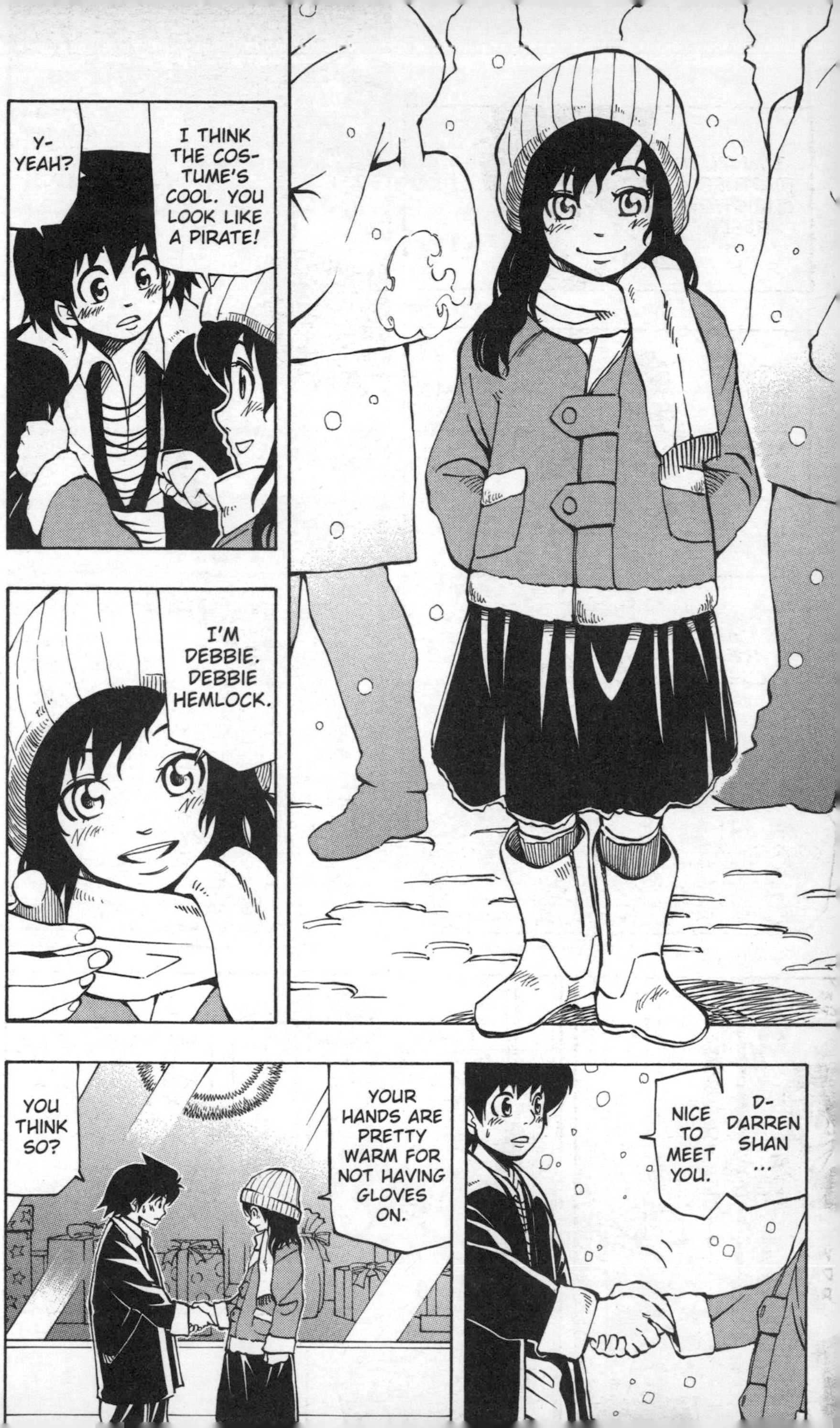
I THINK THE COS-TUME'S COOL. YOU LOOK LIKE A PIRATE!
Y-YEAH?
I'M DEBBIE. DEBBIE HEMLOCK.
D-DARREN SHAN...
NICE TO MEET YOU.
YOUR HANDS ARE PRETTY WARM FOR NOT HAVING GLOVES ON.
YOU THINK SO?

...I MEAN, MY BROTHER A CHRISTMAS PRESENT.

I'M GETTING EV...

WHAT ABOUT YOU?

I LOST *MY* GLOVES EARLIER. THAT'S WHAT I'M HERE TO BUY.

H-HOW DID YOU KNOW?!

OH, THE ONE WITH THE MASK!

I SEE. SO YOU *WEREN'T* JUST TALKING TO A STRANGER.

OF COURSE NOT! HA-HA HA.

I LIVE NEAR HERE, SO I SEE YOU FROM MY WINDOW.

YOU TWO HANG OUT IN THE SQUARE A LOT, DON'T YOU?

KII... (CREEE)

HERE.

WHY, DAR-REN!

I HATE SHOPPING BY MYSELF ANYWAY!

GOOD! IT'S A DEAL, THEN.

#!! (GI... (CREAK)

OKAY...

I CAN HELP YOU LOOK FOR YOUR PRESENT.

WANT TO SHOP TOGETH-ER?

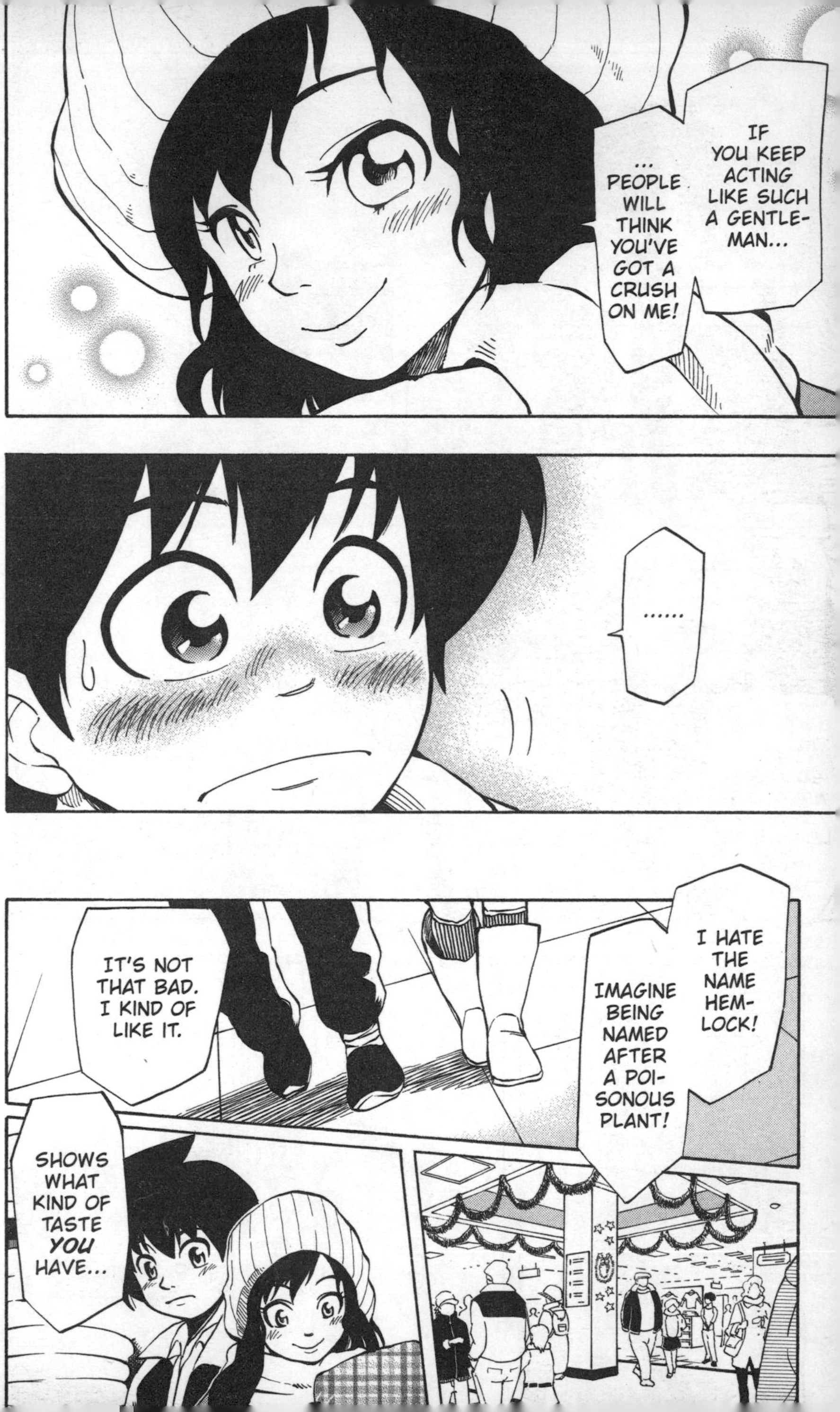
IF YOU KEEP ACTING LIKE SUCH A GENTLE-MAN...
...PEOPLE WILL THINK YOU'VE GOT A CRUSH ON ME!
......
I HATE THE NAME HEM-LOCK!
IMAGINE BEING NAMED AFTER A POI-SONOUS PLANT!
IT'S NOT THAT BAD. I KIND OF LIKE IT.
SHOWS WHAT KIND OF TASTE *YOU* HAVE...

YEAH, ME TOO.

I ONLY JUST RECENTLY MOVED HERE WITH MY PARENTS.

I'M AN ONLY CHILD AND I DON'T HAVE ANY FRIENDS YET, SO I'M GLAD I MET YOU!

W-WELL, HE'S BUSY WITH WORK!

...BUT NEVER YOUR DAD.

WHAT ABOUT YOUR FAMILY? I'VE SEEN YOU WITH YOUR BROTHER A LOT...

I SEE. SO THAT'S WHY YOU'RE ALWAYS LEFT AT THE HOTEL...

THIS BAND IS THE GREATEST!

A CD PLAY-ER!

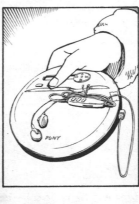

WHAT ABOUT THIS?

NO, I SHOULD BE GOING HOME NOW.

WE'VE STILL GOT TO GET YOUR GLOVES, THOUGH ...

THANKS, DEBBIE! THIS WAS A GREAT PRESENT TO GET HIM.

THE SUN'S ALMOST DOWN.

YOU'RE RIGHT.

IT'S LIKE ONE CITY GOES TO SLEEP AND A NEW ONE WAKES UP.

I LOVE THIS TIME OF EVENING.

REALLY?!

I'LL WALK YOU HOME, DEBBIE.

A CITY WHERE CREATURES OF DARKNESS AWAKE...

THANKS!

AND WE'RE HERE!

WANT TO MEET UP TOMORROW, THEN?

I DON'T HAVE ANY FRIENDS BUT YOU, SO FAR...

BETTER NOT. IT'S LATE. I'M EXPECTED BACK!

DO YOU WANT TO COME IN AND MEET MUM AND DAD?

WHAT ABOUT YOU?

I WON'T HAVE TO START UNTIL THE NEW YEAR.

SURE, BUT WON'T YOU BE AT SCHOOL?

ME TOO!

HA HA HA...

HUH? OH YEAH ...

THERE'S ONE I'VE BEEN DYING TO SEE.

YES! AND A MOVIE TOO!

LET'S GO LOOK FOR YOUR GLOVES TOMORROW, THEN.

WELL ?

TON

TON (TAP)

TATA (TEK TEK)

ASK
...?
ASK
WHAT?

AREN'T YOU GOING TO ASK?

はあ...

HAA...
(CHUFF)

ASK ME TO GO TO A MOVIE!

DUH...

?
?

FUUU
(SIGH)

DAR-
REN!

BUT YOU JUST SAID...

T-THEY DON'T?

DARREN, GIRLS *NEVER* ASK BOYS OUT.

YOU'RE CLUE-LESS, AREN'T YOU?

KUSU (GIGGLE)

? ? ? ?

OKAY?

JUST ASK ME IF I WANT TO GO TO THE MOVIES.

DEBBIE...

MOJI

MOJI (FIDGET)

OKAY, HERE GOES.

......

...WILL YOU COME TO THE MOVIES WITH ME?

WHAT?!

I'LL THINK ABOUT IT.

GACHA (CLICK)

I'M HOOOME!

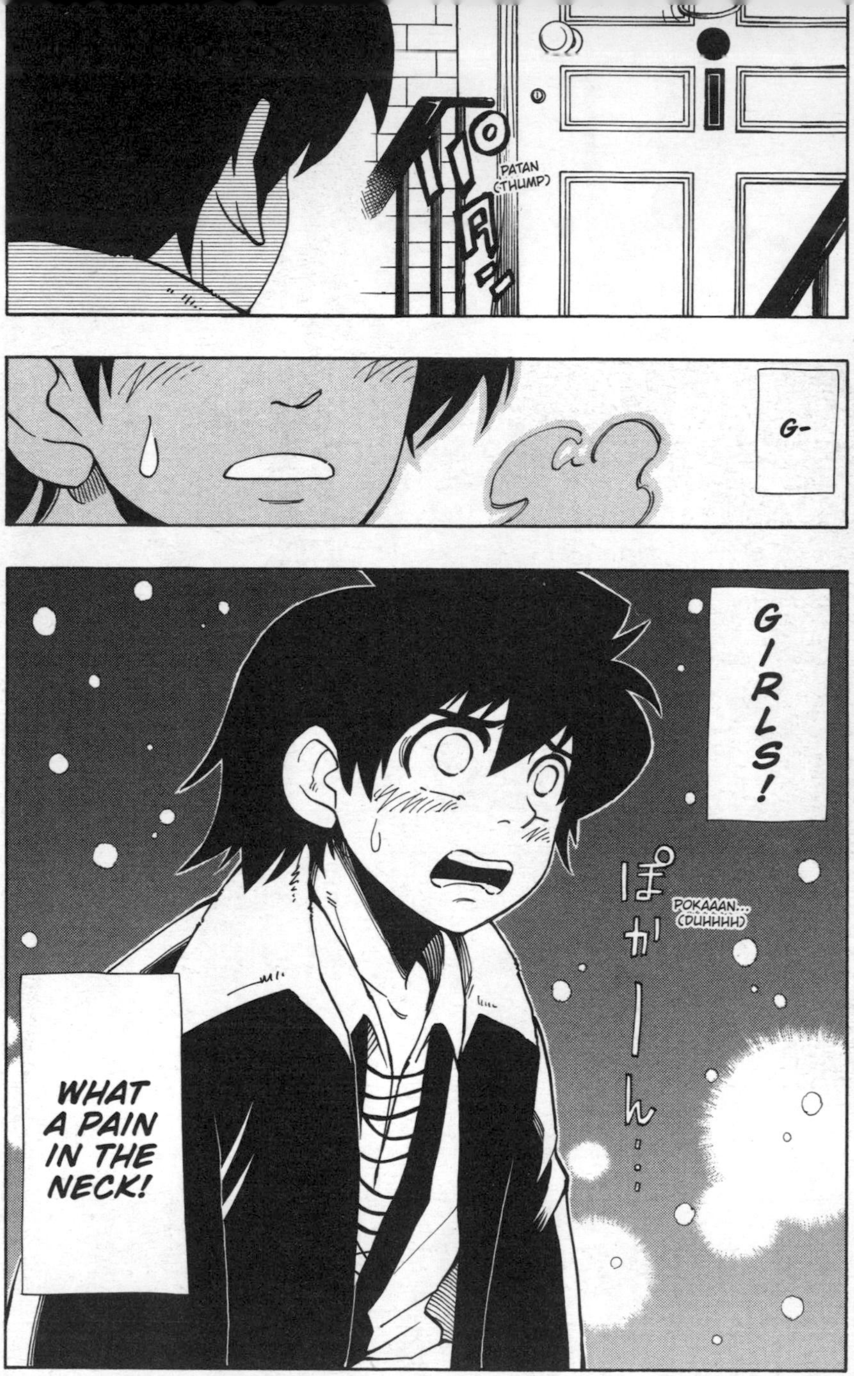
PATAN (THUMP)
G-
GIRLS!
ぽかーん…
POKAAAN… (DUHHHH)
WHAT A PAIN IN THE NECK!

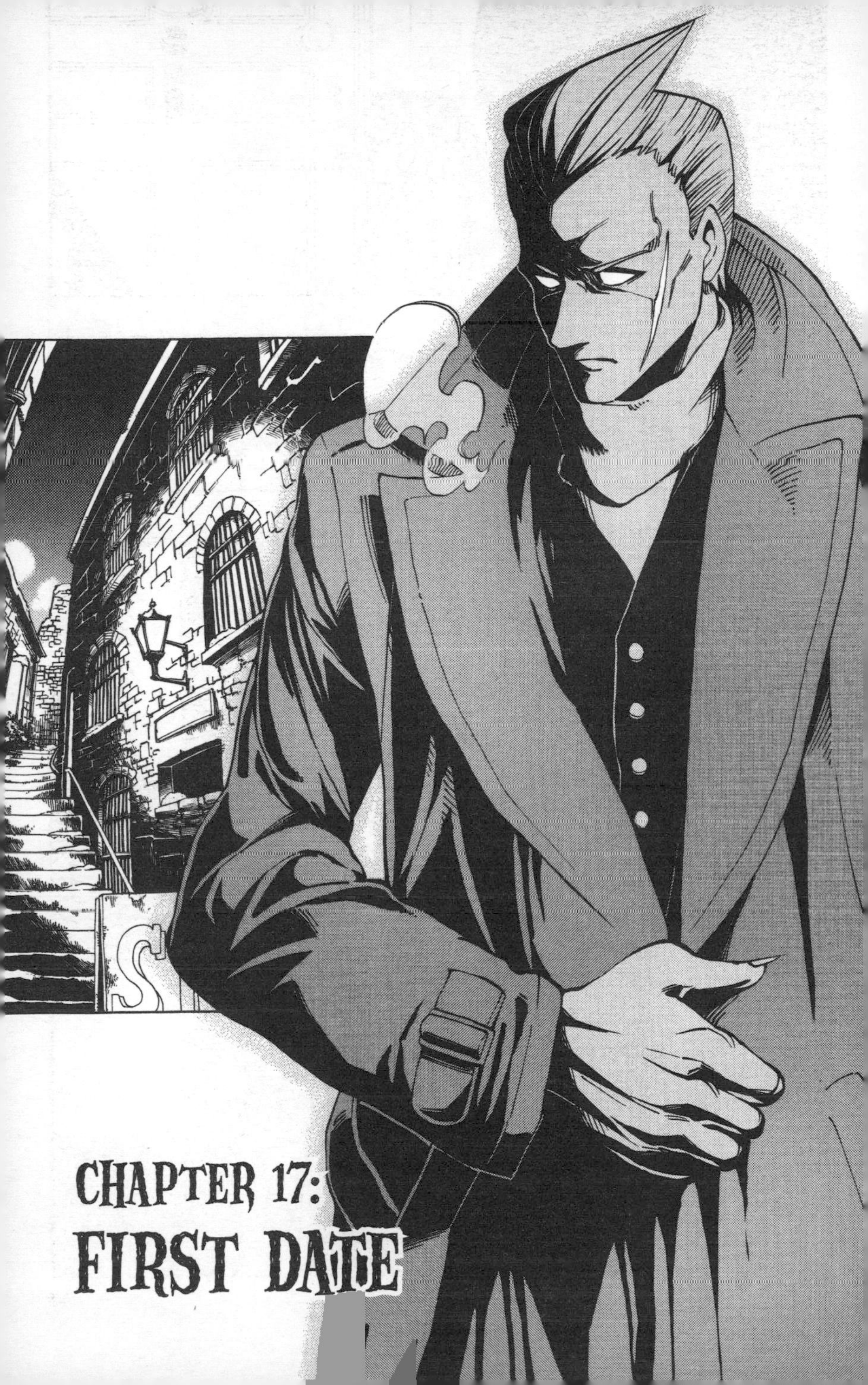
CHAPTER 17:
FIRST DATE

QUIET, EVRA! MR. CREPSLEY'S STILL SLEEPING.

IT'S NEARLY TIME FOR YOUR DATE, DARREN!

I'VE NEVER BEEN ON A DATE.

DOES THIS LOOK FINE?

YOU KNOW YOU'RE EXCITED!

IT'S NOT A DATE, JUST THE MOVIES.

I WISH *I* HAD A DATE.

NO, THAT DOESN'T COUNT!

SEE? YOU JUST ADMITTED IT WAS A DATE!

!!

GIVE HER A KISS!

MUCHUU (SMOOCH)

GABA (GRAB)

AND THEN?

CHAT WITH HER. TELL A FEW JOKES...

DON'T WORRY! JUST ACT NORMAL.

GACHA (CLICK)

CAN I FIX YOU SOMETHING TO EAT?

YOU'RE AWAKE, MR. CREPSLEY!

OH!

MR. CREPSLEY!

NO. I MUST BE GOING IMMEDIATELY...

WHAT? OH...

DON'T WORRY ABOUT ME! HAVE FUN!

WELL, I SHOULD BE GOING. I'LL BE BACK BEFORE TOO LONG.

IS HE ALL RIGHT? HE SEEMS PREOCCUPIED WITH *SOMETHING...* I'M WORRIED ABOUT HIM.

BATAN (SLAM)

GACHA
(CLICK)
ガチャ

THANKS FOR WAITING. SHALL WE GO?

YEAH!

SHANTA

VAMPIRE BABE

ANTA

VAMPIRE BABE

...WE WENT TO SEE A MOVIE, AS PLANNED.

AFTER WE FOUND DEBBIE A NICE PAIR OF GLOVES...

I WASN'T IMPRESSED WITH THE FAKENESS OF THE MONSTERS AND GHOSTS IN THE FILM...

BLAM BLAM

KUA (YAWN)

...BUT DEBBIE ENJOYED IT A LOT MORE THAN ME.

Wa-H

THE MOVIE WAS ONE OF THOSE POPULAR COMEDIC HORROR FILMS.

KLANG SWAK

SFX: BURU (SHIVER)

Y-YOU SCARED?

DOKI (THUMP)

DOKI

GYUUU

GYU (SQUEEZE)

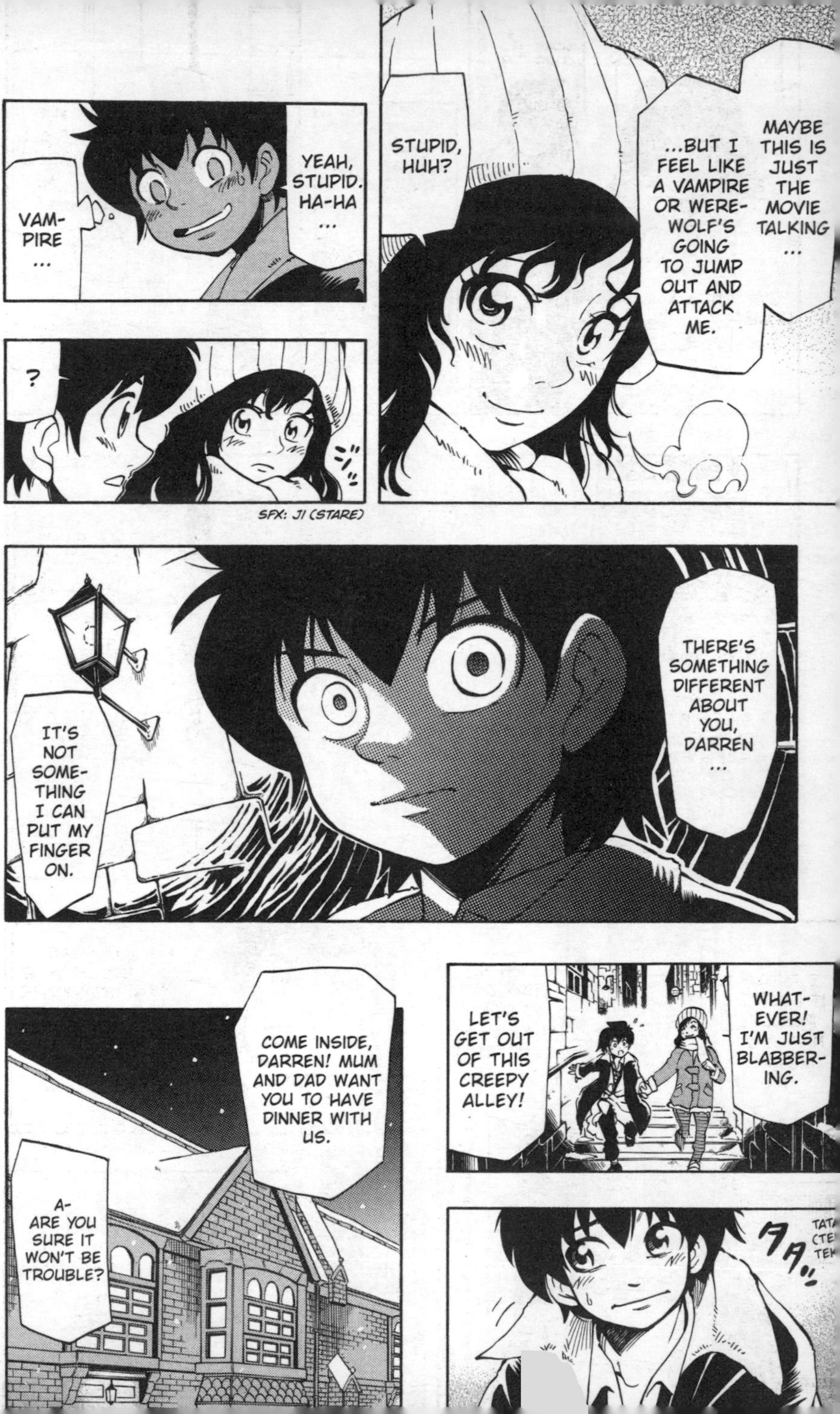
MAYBE THIS IS JUST THE MOVIE TALKING ...
...BUT I FEEL LIKE A VAMPIRE OR WERE-WOLF'S GOING TO JUMP OUT AND ATTACK ME.
STUPID, HUH?
YEAH, STUPID. HA-HA ...
VAM-PIRE ...
?
SFX: JI (STARE)
THERE'S SOMETHING DIFFERENT ABOUT YOU, DARREN ...
IT'S NOT SOME-THING I CAN PUT MY FINGER ON.
WHAT-EVER! I'M JUST BLABBER-ING.
LET'S GET OUT OF THIS CREEPY ALLEY!
COME INSIDE, DARREN! MUM AND DAD WANT YOU TO HAVE DINNER WITH US.
A- ARE YOU SURE IT WON'T BE TROUBLE?

PATAN
(CLICK)

I'M HOME!

W-WELL, IF YOU SAY SO...

NOT AT ALL. COME IN!

SFX: DO (THUMP) DO

I WAS EVEN MORE NERVOUS THAN THE TIME I STOLE MADAM OCTA FROM MR. CREPSLEY...

...BUT I NEEDN'T HAVE BEEN. DEBBIE'S PARENTS WERE JUST AS NICE AS SHE WAS.

I THINK IT LOOKS REALLY NICE AND CLEAN.

IT'S NOT VERY GIRLY. I DON'T LIKE BEING CLUTTERED.

HER DAD, JESSE, WAS A COMPUTER EXPERT WHO HAD TO MOVE AROUND A LOT FOR HIS WORK.

HER MUM, DONNA, WAS A FORMER CHEF, AND HER COOKING WAS EX-CELLENT.

WE CAN DECORATE TOGETHER.

COME OVER FOR CHRISTMAS EVE, DARREN! YOU CAN BRING YOUR BROTHER AND DAD.

I'M GOING TO DECORATE IT ON CHRISTMAS EVE!

WHAT'S WITH THE MINI CHRISTMAS TREE?

... SURE.

THE NIGHT PASSED QUICKLY, AND THEN...

WHOEVER SAID, "TIME FLIES WHEN YOU'RE HAVING FUN," WAS RIGHT.

YES! IT'S JUST... UM...

DON'T YOU WANT TO KISS ME?

K-K-KISS?!

IT'S TIME FOR ME TO GO.

DON'T I GET A GOOD-NIGHT KISS?

C-CAN'T I SAY GOODBYE TO YOUR PARENTS?

I'LL SHOW YOU OUT.

TON (TEP)

TON

I... UH...

I DON'T CARE ONE WAY OR THE OTHER.

HEY, FORGET IT.

ガチャ... GACHA (CLICK)

ONLY, BE A LITTLE BRAVER, OKAY?

OKAY, YOU CAN COME OVER TOMORROW. I WANT YOU TO!

KUSU (GIGGLE)

Y-YEAH... THAT'S IT.

......

SURE, IF YOU WANT TO.

CAN I COME OVER TOMORROW?

SCARED?

LOOK, DEBBIE, I'M SORRY I DIDN'T KISS YOU. I'M JUST ...

PATAN
(THUMP)

TO-
MOR-
ROW
THEN.

OKAY
...

KON
(TAP)

KON

コン
コン

DARREN!
WHAT
ARE YOU
DOING?

?

E
E
K
!

THIS IS THE SECOND FLOOR! HOW...?

GUGU (GRRG)

HEH-HEH, I'M FLOATING ON AIR.

...THE OFFER OF A KISS.

YOU KNOW...

IS THE OFFER STILL ON?

I CLIMBED UP BE- CAUSE... WELL...

WHAT OFFER?

COME IN, QUICK, BEFORE YOU—

YOU'RE CRAZY! YOU'LL SLIP AND FALL.

I DON'T WANT TO COME IN.

YOU COULD HAVE KNOCKED ON THE DOOR.

YOU'RE REALLY CRAZY.

YOU WENT TO ALL THIS TROUBLE JUST FOR THAT?

I DIDN'T THINK OF THAT.

OH YEAH!

KOKU (NOD)

KUSU KUSU (CHEE)

HA (HA) HA

DO DO DO (THUMP)

ALL RIGHT!

DOKI (THUMP)

DOKI

BUT QUICKLY, OKAY?

I SUPPOSE YOU DESERVE ONE.

Y-YES.

DO (THUD)

DO

DOK! DOK! (THUMP)

WORTH COMING UP FOR?

WELL?

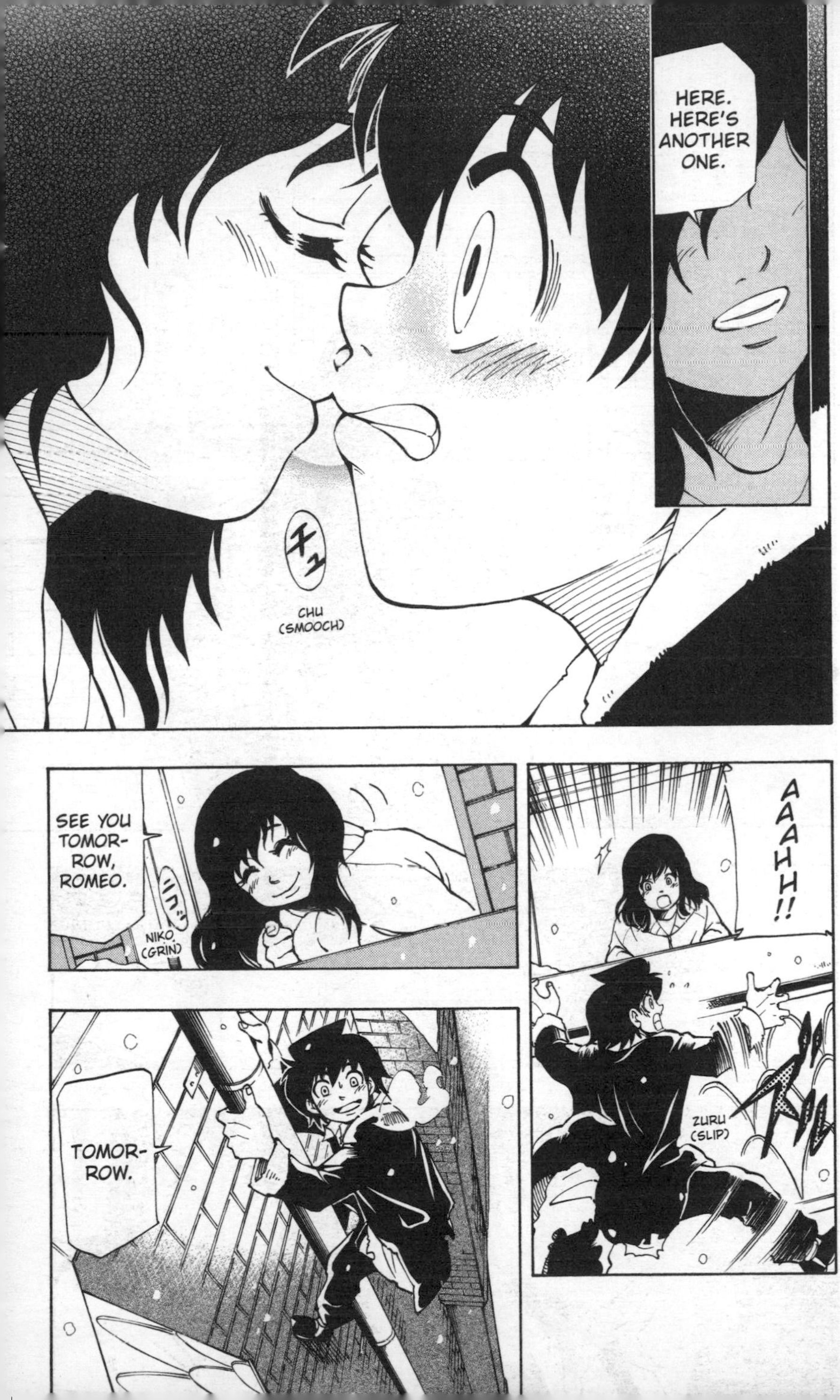
HERE. HERE'S ANOTHER ONE.
チュ
CHU (SMOOCH)
SEE YOU TOMORROW, ROMEO.
ニコッ
NIKO (GRIN)
AAAHH!!
ZURU (SLIP)
TOMORROW.

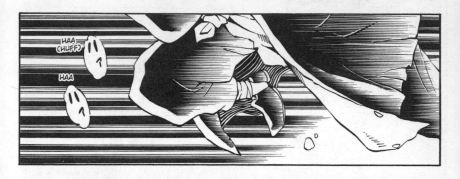

LISTEN, EVRA! YOU WON'T BELIEVE WHAT HAPPENED TONIGHT!

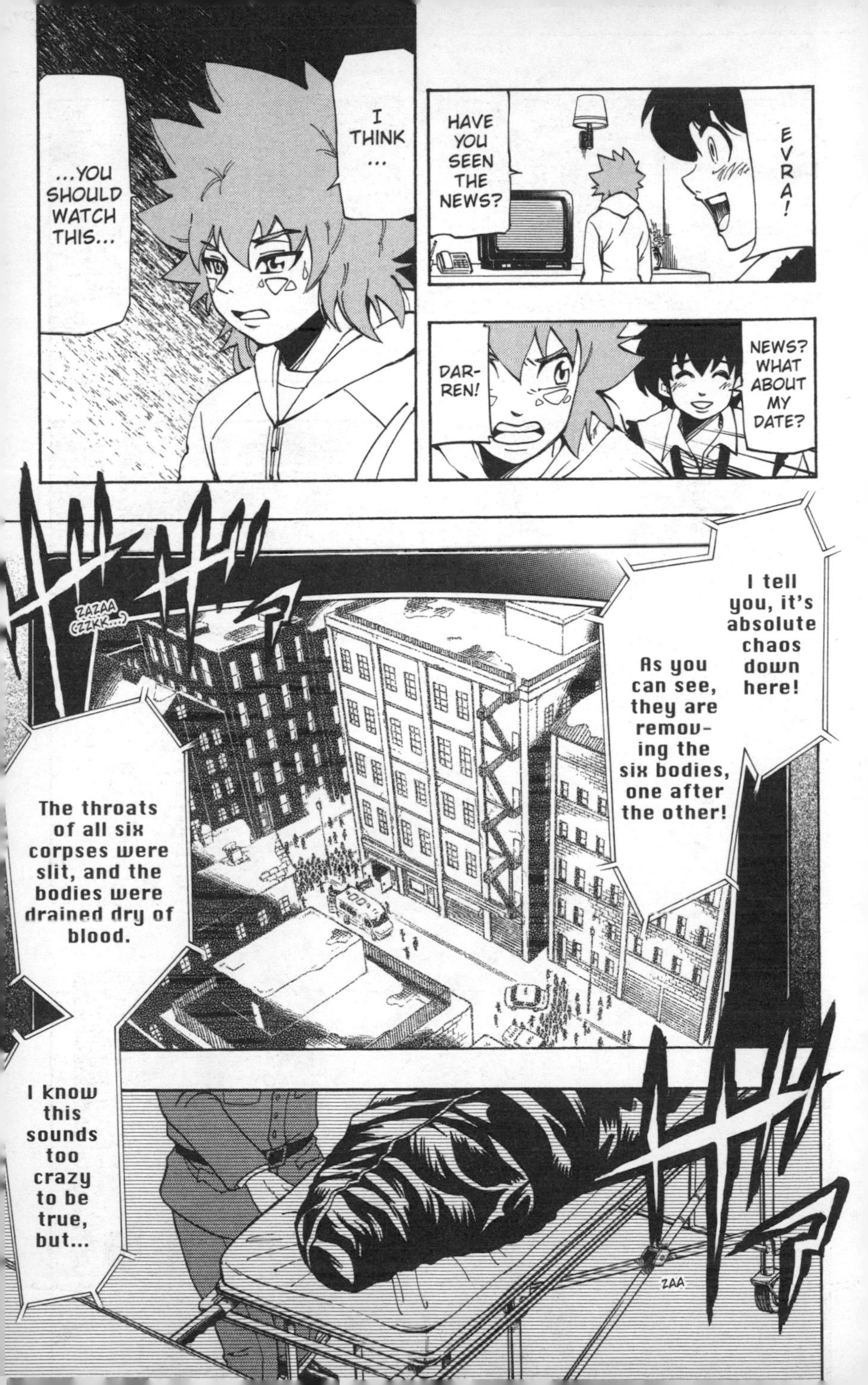
EVRA!
HAVE YOU SEEN THE NEWS?
NEWS? WHAT ABOUT MY DATE?
DARREN!
I THINK...
...YOU SHOULD WATCH THIS...
ZAZAA (ZZKK...)
I tell you, it's absolute chaos down here!
As you can see, they are removing the six bodies, one after the other!
The throats of all six corpses were slit, and the bodies were drained dry of blood.
I know this sounds too crazy to be true, but...
ZAA

...it's almost like they've been killed by a VAMPIRE!

...BACK YET.

HE'S NOT...

The bodies appear to be several days dead...

EVRA... WHERE'S MR. CREPSLEY?

THE KILLER... COULD IT BE... MR. CREPSLEY?!

CHAPTER 18:
SUSPICIOUS MINDS

How's it look, Evra? Can you see him?

WE'VE GOT BINOCULARS AND CELL PHONES.

Plain as day!

YEAH.

Let's find out what Mr. Crepsley's been up to!

HOW COULD I HAVE IMAGINED THINGS COMING TO THIS?

58

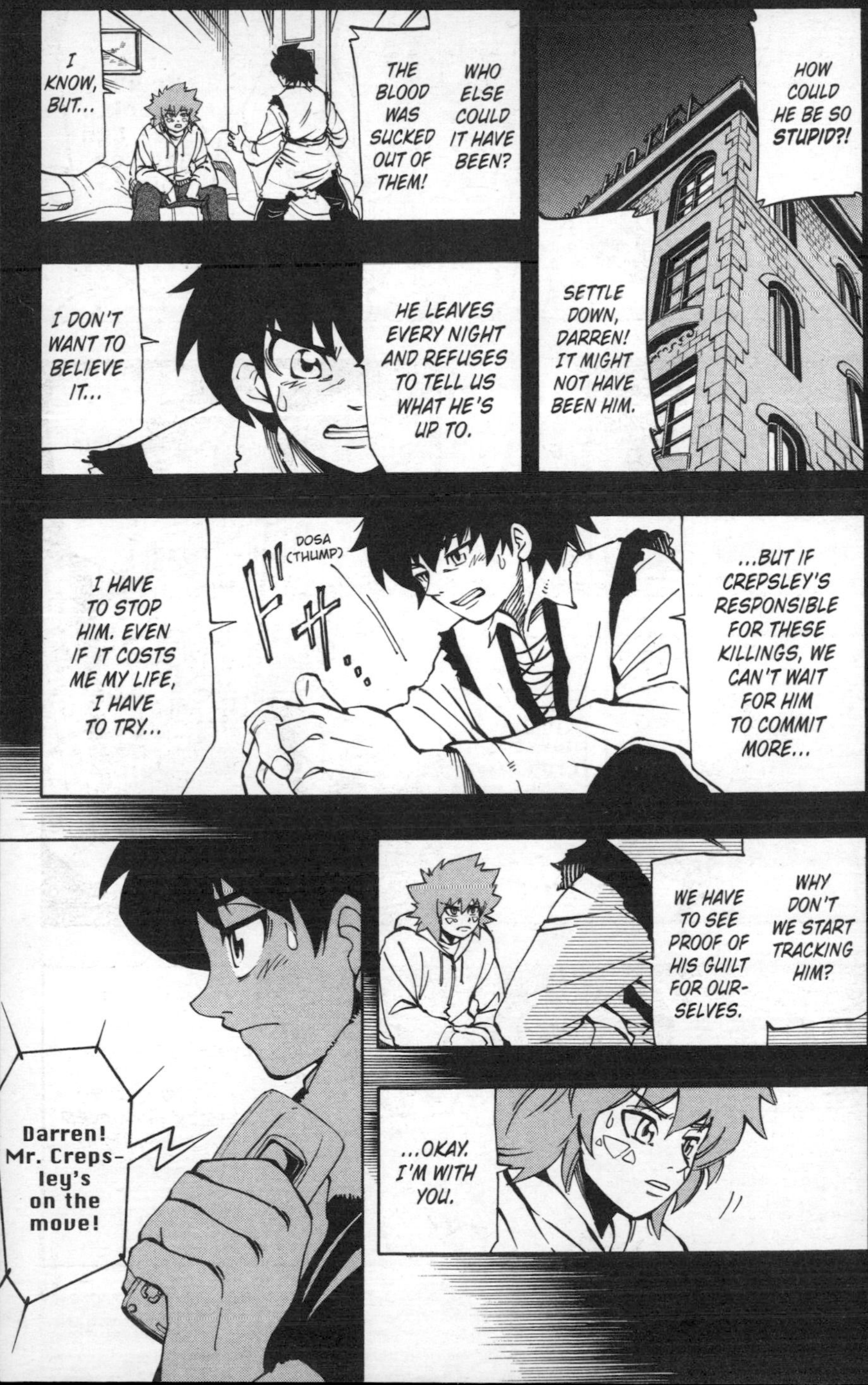

HOW COULD HE BE SO STUPID?!
SETTLE DOWN, DARREN! IT MIGHT NOT HAVE BEEN HIM.
WHO ELSE COULD IT HAVE BEEN?
THE BLOOD WAS SUCKED OUT OF THEM!
I KNOW, BUT...
HE LEAVES EVERY NIGHT AND REFUSES TO TELL US WHAT HE'S UP TO.
I DON'T WANT TO BELIEVE IT...
...BUT IF CREPSLEY'S RESPONSIBLE FOR THESE KILLINGS, WE CAN'T WAIT FOR HIM TO COMMIT MORE...
ドサ
DOSA (THUMP)
I HAVE TO STOP HIM. EVEN IF IT COSTS ME MY LIFE, I HAVE TO TRY...
WHY DON'T WE START TRACKING HIM?
WE HAVE TO SEE PROOF OF HIS GUILT FOR OUR-SELVES.
...OKAY. I'M WITH YOU.
Darren! Mr. Creps-ley's on the move!

JI
(ZZT...)

FU
(FSH)

URO
(STEP)

URO

!!?

HE
VANISHED
!!

I really doubt it.

YOU DON'T THINK HE NOTICED WE WERE TRACKING HIM, DO YOU?

HE WAS TOO FAST FOR ME TO SEE WHICH WAY HE WENT...

Did you see that, Darren?

...BUT FROM THIS DISTANCE, PLUS BEING DOWNWIND...

VAMPIRES MIGHT HAVE VERY SHARP SENSES...

YOU'RE RIGHT...

WE'LL HAVE TO TRY AGAIN TOMORROW...

DA (DASH)

WE FAILED HELPLESSLY ON OUR FIRST TWO NIGHTS OF FOLLOWING MR. CREPSLEY.

BUT WE STUCK WITH IT AND GOT BETTER AT KEEPING UP WITH HIM.

AND THERE WEREN'T ANY NEW VICTIMS... YET.

MOGU (MPH)

MOGU

5

FU
(WHISH)

IN THE LAST FEW NIGHTS, WE'VE LEARNED THAT MR. CREPSLEY HAS TWO MAIN PATTERNS.

GONE AGAIN!

BA
(LEAP)

GOT IT!

I saw him descend to the street! I'll follow him!

...OR HE RESTLESSLY PROWLS THE STREETS BELOW.

HE EITHER STANDS ABOVE AND SILENTLY WATCHES THE CROWDS BENEATH HIM...

LOOKING FOR HIS NEXT VICTIM?

AS IF HE'S LOOKING FOR SOMEONE...

SASA
(SHHH)

KYORO
(SPIN)

KYORO
キョロ

キョロ

MUKURI (SHLUMP)

THE ALL-NIGHT STALKING WAS MAKING ME SLEEP LIKE A ROCK...

...BUT I STILL MADE TIME FOR DEBBIE.

SUU (ZZZ)

SUU

HOTEL

HA (GASP)

KUSU (GIGGLE)

I KNOW I'M STILL A HALF-VAMPIRE.

THOSE BAGS UNDER YOUR EYES! ARE YOU OKAY?

I KNOW THIS ISN'T THE MOST SENSIBLE THING I COULD BE DOING.

I KNOW THIS ISN'T GOING TO LAST FOREVER.

SHALL WE GO?

UTO (DOZE)

UTO

BEING WITH MY VERY FIRST GIRLFRIEND IS MORE IMPORTANT TO ME THAN ANYTHING.

BUT I LOVE SPENDING TIME WITH HER.

HYUUUUU
(WHOOOOSH)

PIKU
(TWIK)

ZUSHA
(THMMP)

HYU
(ZSHHH)

!?

SU
(SHK)

SU

HAVE YOU PICKED UP ON THIS, DARREN?

Yeah, you too?

YEAH. HE'S FOLLOWING THIS FAT GUY.

GOKU
(GULP)

MR. CREPSLEY'S ACTING DIFFERENTLY TONIGHT.

GAYA

GAYA
(HUSTLE)

GAYA

COULD THIS BE THE NEXT TARGET OF MR. CREPSLEY'S KILLING SPREE?

Is he going to wait for the man to come back out?

He's just sitting there.

MAYBE.

FUU (HFF)

SU (SHH)

What kind of factory is it?

I SMELL FISH BLOOD ...

MUST BE A FISH PROCESSING PLANT.

OKAY.

I'LL COME AND JOIN YOU.

It could be a long wait.

NOPE...

WHEWWW. NO MOVES YET?

IN FACT, MY NERVES ARE SO TENSE, THEY'RE KEEPING ME WARM.

I'M A VAMPIRE— I CAN HANDLE COLD BETTER THAN YOU.

BURU (SHIVER)

HAA (HUFF)

BURU

HUH? NO! WON'T YOU BE COLD?

YOU SHOULD WEAR MY COAT, EVRA.

!

BA (ZIP)

THANKS, DARREN.

......

PIKUN (TWITCH)

HE'S COMING BACK OUT!

SUKU (RISE)

SU

SU (SHH)

WHY? DID HE NOTICE US?!

CREPSLEY'S COMING THIS WAY!

OH, CRAP!

W-WHAT'S WRONG?!

WE'VE GOT TO MOVE!

NO, HE'S FOLLOWING THE MAN!

NO, THERE'S NO TIME!

GABA (THWUMP)

DON'T EVEN BREATHE!

KEEP PERFECTLY STILL!

DO

DO

DO (BUMP)

DO

DOKI

DOKI (BA-BUMP)

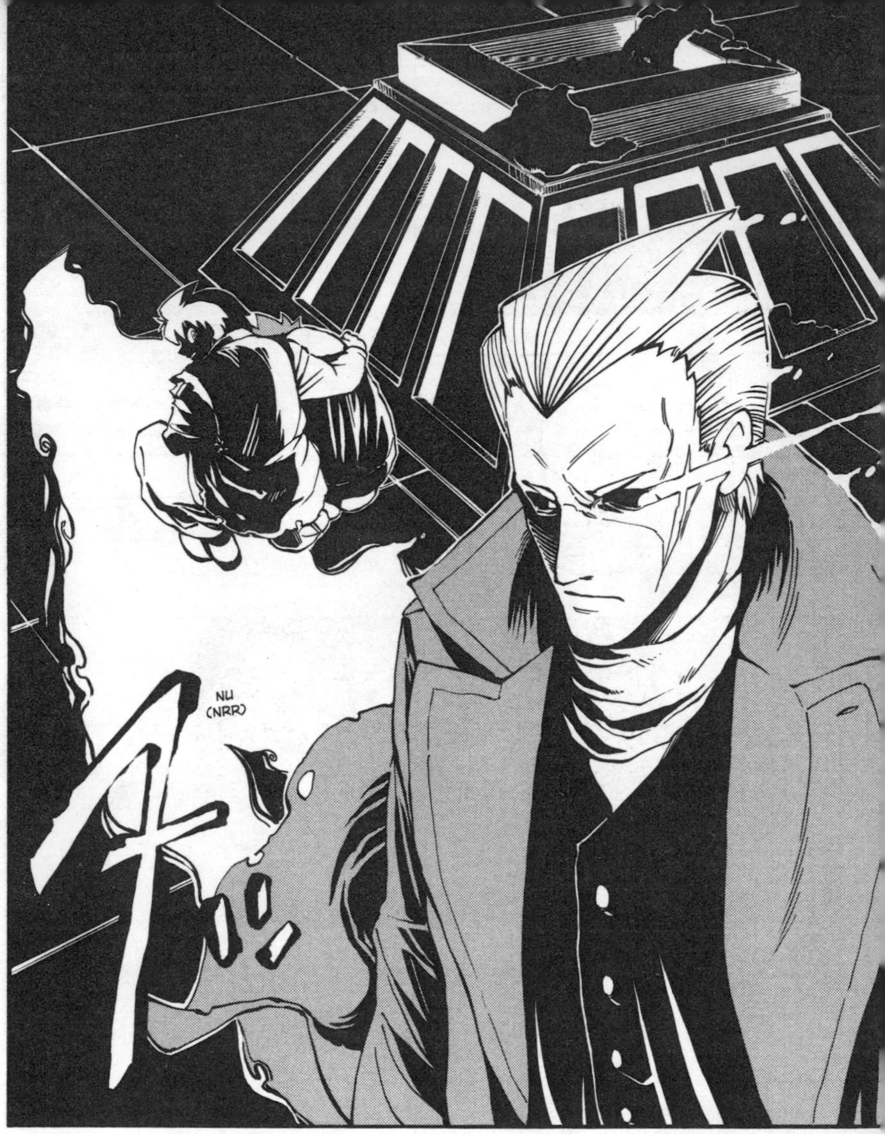
NU
(NRR)

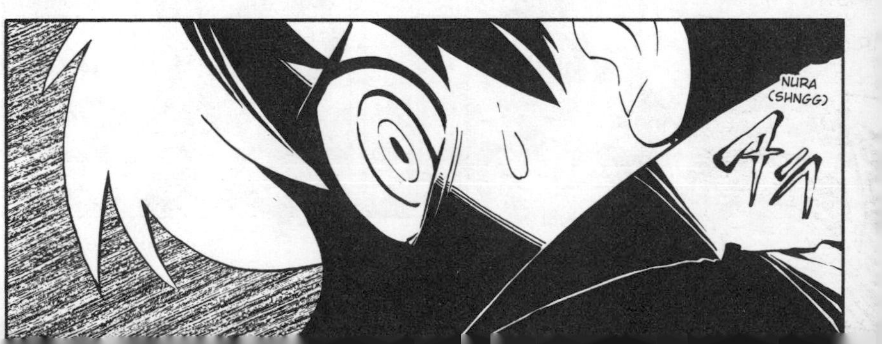
NURA
(SHNGG)

PURU
プル

PURU (SHIVER)
プル

......

DO
ド

DO (BA-BUMP)
ド

HYU
(SWISH)

I THINK MY HEART STOPPED!

GASP!!

HE'S WAY TOO FOCUSED ON THAT MAN!

SOMETHING'S WRONG. MR. CREPSLEY WOULD EASILY HAVE NOTICED US, NORMALLY.

ALL RIGHT, ALL RIGHT!

WE'VE GOT TO FOLLOW THEM!

DA (DSHH)

LET'S GO, EVRA!

HE'S OBVIOUSLY GOING TO KILL THAT GUY!

THERE'S NO TIME TO THINK ABOUT THIS!

WE CAN'T! WE'RE UN-ARMED AND HELPLESS!

WHAT IF THAT MAN ENDS UP DEAD TOO?

HAS TO BE...

YOU THINK THAT'S HIS HOUSE?

HUH?!

WE'VE **GOT** TO STOP HIM BEFORE HE CAN DO IT!

ONCE MR. CREPSLEY GOES INTO THE BUILDING, WE'RE MOVING IN!

MIGHT AS WELL GO FOR BROKE THEN.

DO (BA-BUMP)

DO

READY, SET...

DO

KYORO (SPIN)

KYORO

DOKI (BA-BUMP)

HERE WE GO...

DOKI

SU (STOK)

SU

......!?

GUGUGU... (CHRGGG)

WHAT'S WRONG, DARREN? NOT YET?

KURU (SPIN)

HUH ?!

HE LEFT...

I'M NOT SURE...

WHY THE SUDDEN CHANGE OF HEART, I WON-DER?

ズルッ ーZURU! (SLIDE)

WHEW... HA-HA, I'M GLAD.

WAS IT *REALLY MR. CREPSLEY* WHO KILLED THOSE PEOPLE?

I DON'T KNOW... I JUST DON'T KNOW...

IT'S OBVIOUS THAT THE MAN IS HIS OBJECTIVE.

BUT HE HASN'T MADE A MOVE YET...

IT'S THE SECOND NIGHT SINCE MR. CREPSLEY STARTED STALKING THE MAN WORKING AT THE FISH FACTORY...

CHAPTER 19:
A MYSTERIOUS CREATURE

THE CITY IS DECKED OUT FOR CHRISTMAS.

TODAY IS DECEMBER 21ST.

STILL STARING AT THE FACTORY, AS USUAL.

WHAT'S MR. CREPSLEY DOING?

WHAT IF HE ATTACKS? DO WE STAND A CHANCE AGAINST HIM IN A FIGHT?

YOU AND ME...

HE MUST BE WAITING FOR THE RIGHT MOMENT TO KILL THE MAN...

I WONDER WHAT HE'S PLOTTING.

GOSO
(SHFF)

I FOUND IT WHILE WALKING AROUND THE FACTORY LAST NIGHT.

IT'S RUSTY, BUT IT'LL MAKE DO FOR A WEAPON.

HEY, WHERE'D YOU GET THAT?!

GIRA
(GINGG)

76

I ONLY AGREED TO GO ALONG WITH MR. CREPSLEY BECAUSE HE CONVINCED ME HE WASN'T BAD.

PLUS, THIS IS MY PROB- LEM.

YES... BUT IT HAS TO BE ME ALONE.

I DON'T WANT YOU IN- VOLVED, EVRA.

YOU'RE SURE ABOUT THIS?

I BELIEVED THAT VAMPIRES DIDN'T KILL INNOCENT PEOPLE.

YOU'RE NOT A VAMPIRE. YOU WOULDN'T LAST A SECOND...

NO WAY!

IF HE'S ABOUT TO COMMIT HIS SEVENTH MURDER, I'LL MAKE SURE HE DOESN'T.

I HAVE TO SEE FOR MYSELF.

IF HE'S REALLY THE ONE RESPONSIBLE FOR THE DEATHS OF THOSE SIX PEOPLE, I CAN'T STAY WITH HIM ANYMORE.

OKAY, YOU WIN...

...

EVRA ...

LET'S STOP HIM TOGETH- ER!

YOU CAN'T TAKE THIS ALL ON YOURSELF!

SORRY, GO ON AHEAD. I'LL CATCH UP!

HURRY UP, DARREN! WE'LL LOSE SIGHT OF MR. CREPSLEY!

ALL RIGHT. CALL MY MOBILE!

GOSO GOSO (RUSTLE)

BUT IT NEVER HAPPENED...

SU (SHH)

..."LET'S GO BACK TO THE CIRQUE DU FREAK."

EVERY NIGHT, I FERVENTLY HOPED FOR MR. CREPSLEY TO SHOW UP AND SAY...

FINALLY, THE NIGHT OF THE 22ND...

...MR. CREPS-LEY TOOK ACTION.

SHA (WHISK)

!!

THIS IS IT...

GAKON (THUK)

KOKUN (NOD)

SOOO...
(SNEAK)

HIRA
(FLIP)

SASA
(SHWIP)

GAGAGAGA
(VRRRRR)

POCHI
(POP)

...IT'S BEEN NICE KNOWING YOU, EVRA VON.

DARREN...

AND IF I FAIL...

YOU WAIT HERE, EVRA.

SU (SHP)

I HAVEN'T HAD THE CHANCE TO TEACH YOU ABOUT CHRISTMAS YET...

...LOOK IN THE DRAWERS AT THE HOTEL.

ON THE CHANCE I DON'T COME BACK...

GOOD LUCK.

BE CAREFUL.

TON (TAP)

GASHAN (CLANK)

ZUSHA (ZSHHH)

THAT'S ALL I'M SAYING! BE BACK IN A BIT!

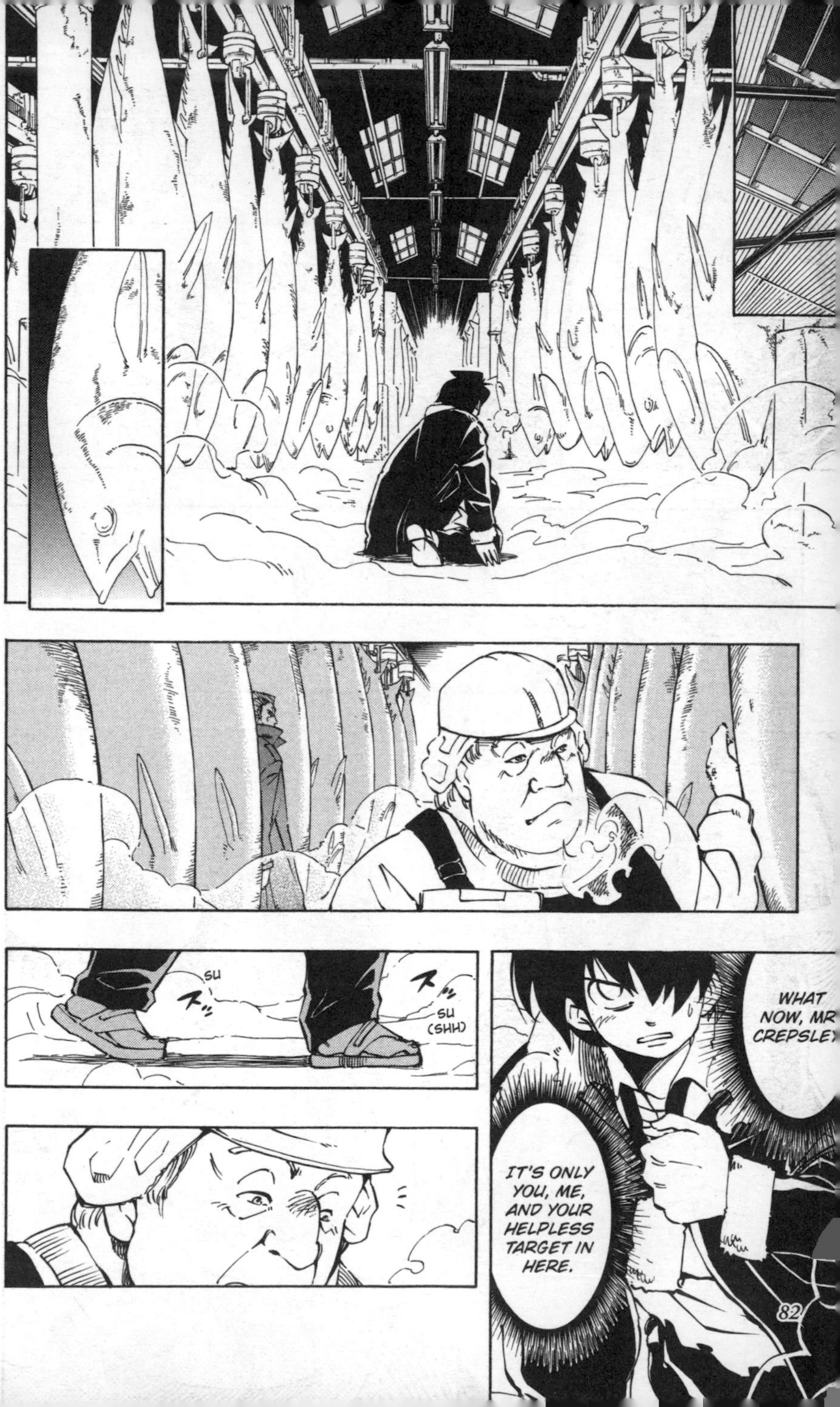
SU
ス
SU
(SHH)
ス
WHAT NOW, MR CREPSLE
IT'S ONLY YOU, ME, AND YOUR HELPLESS TARGET IN HERE.

DON'T DO IT...

NO, MR. CREPSLEY!

HYU (WHUF)

SU

SU (SHH)

CHI (TSK)

SFX: DO (BA-BUMP) DO

THERE! BEHIND YOU!

NO...

TOO LATE!!!

DAN
(DSHH)

SHA
(SHHK)

AAAAAAAH!!!

BIKU
(HRK)

DON
(THUD)

WHY ARE YOU HERE?!

DARREN?!

BI
(SLASH)

FUUU

FUUU
(CHUFF)

I WON'T LET YOU KILL THIS POOR MAN...

ZUDAN
(STOMP)

AAAH!!

ZUSHA (SK-
SHH)

GASHAAAAN
(KRAAASHHH)

IF YOU WANT TO GET AT HIM, YOU'LL HAVE TO COME THROUGH ME!!!

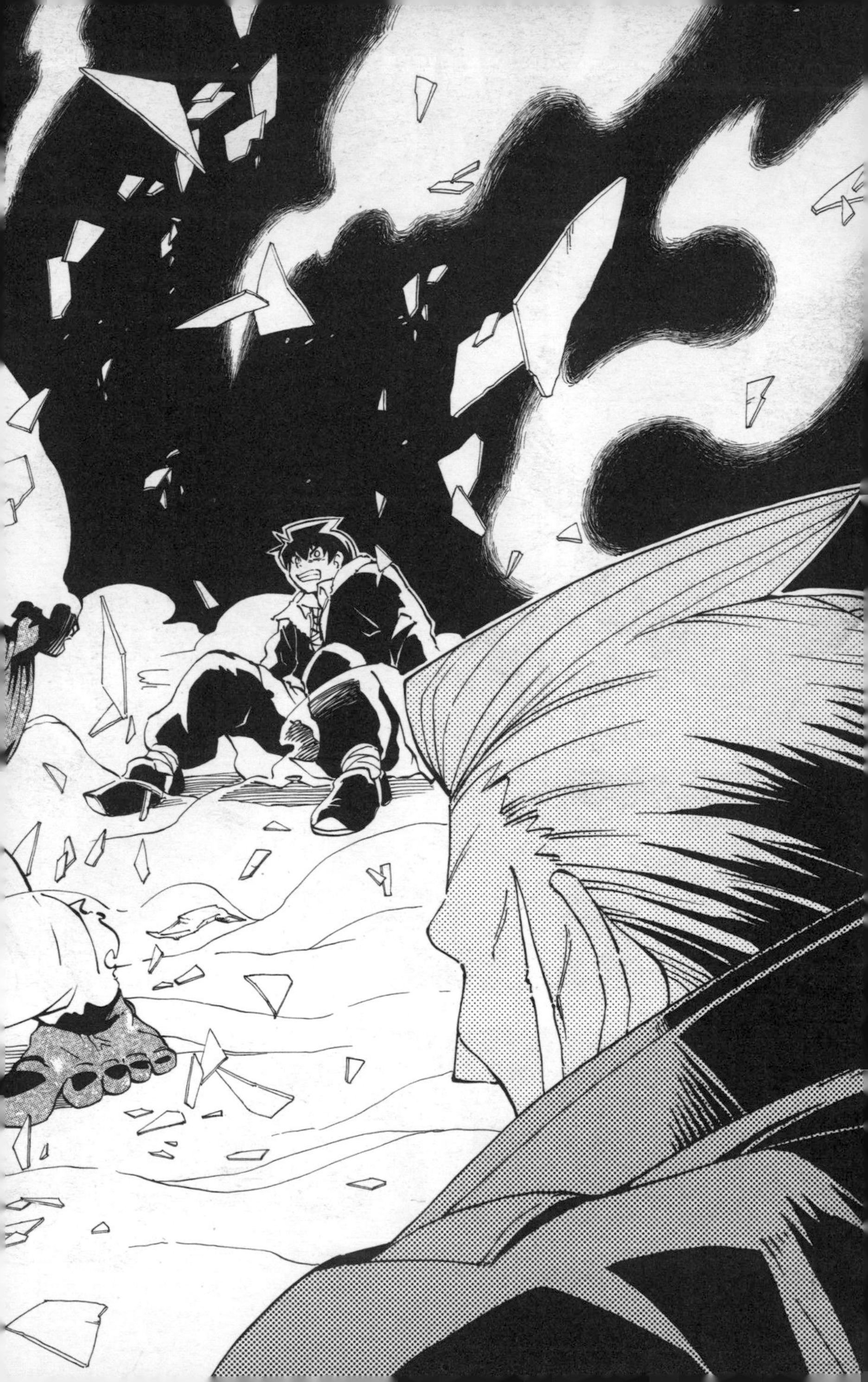

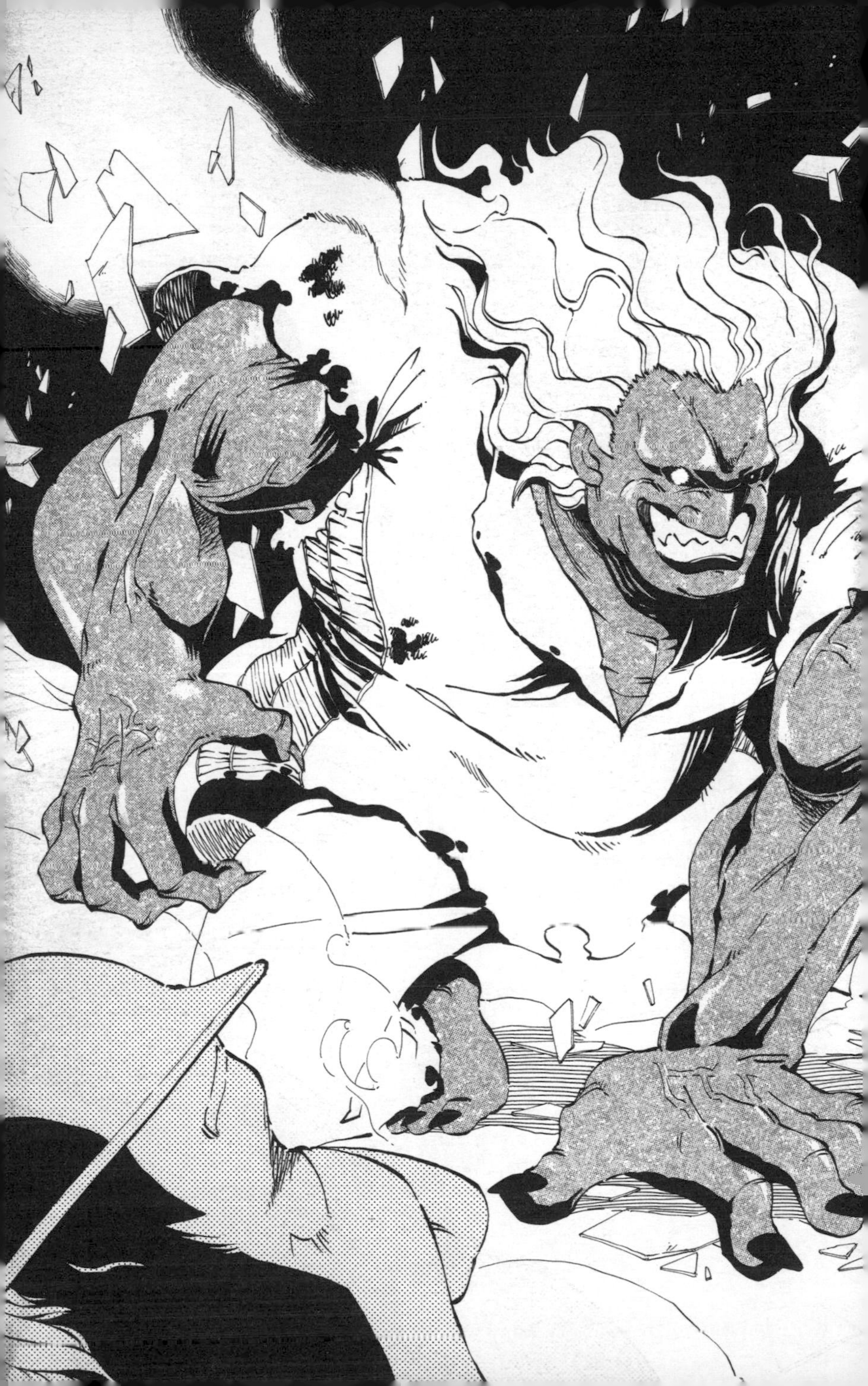

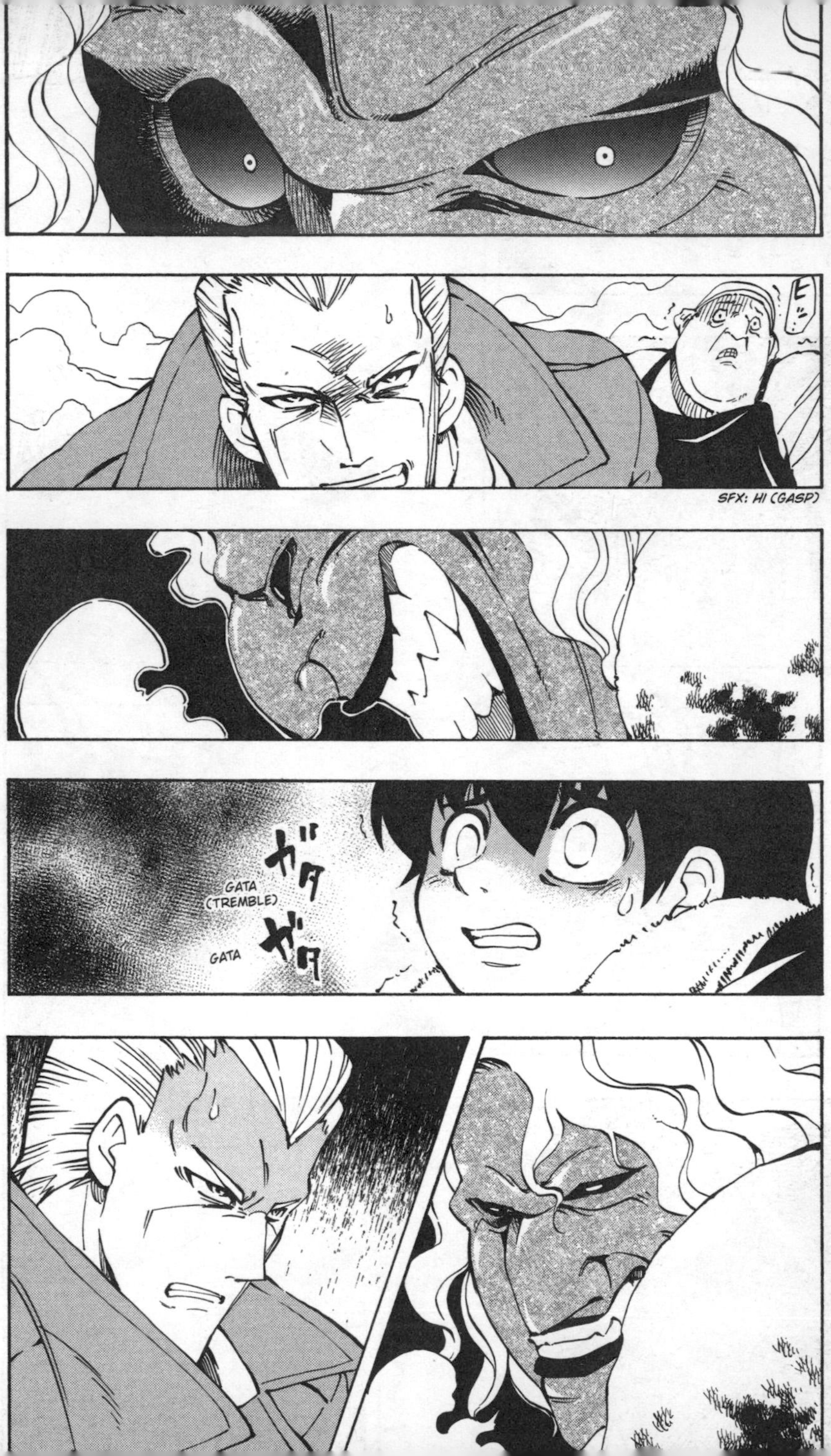
SFX: HI (GASP)
ガタ
GATA (TREMBLE)
ガタ
GATA

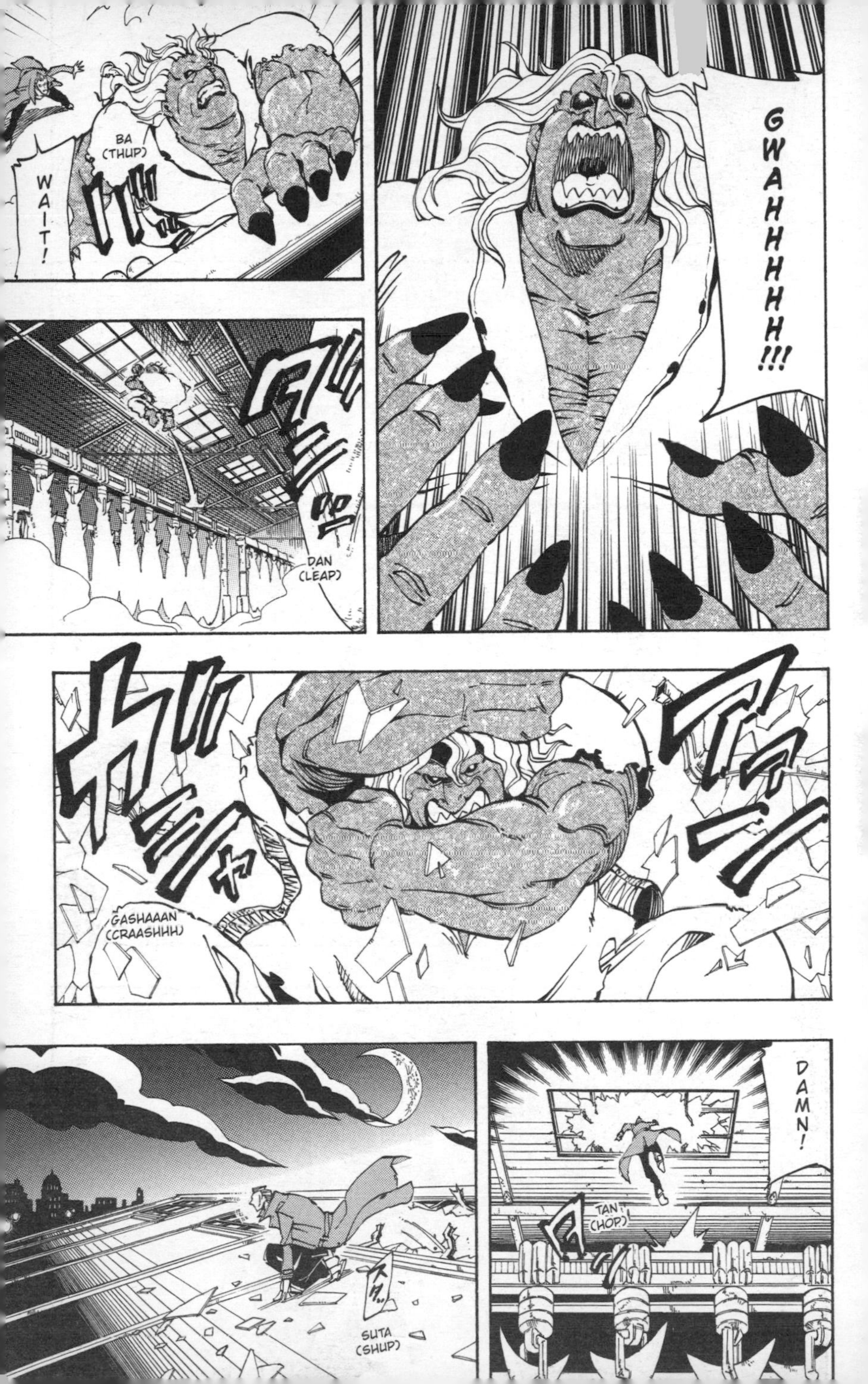
GWAHHHHHH!!!
BA (THUP)
WAIT!
DAN (LEAP)
GASHAAAN (CRAASHHH)
DAMN!
TAN (HOP)
SUTA (SHUP)

HI HII
HI
(SOB)

GAKU
(SLUMP)

CHI
(TSK)

ZURU
ZURU
(SKRP)

FUU...
(PUFF)

NO,
MR.
CREPS-
LEY!

FUWA
(FFP)

TSUKA
(TKK)

TSUKA

ZZ
ZZ

SUUU
(ZZZ)

SUUU
(ZZZ)

GOTO
(THUD)

GIRO
(GRR)

DO YOU REALIZE WHAT YOU HAVE DONE?!

DO YOU!!?

YOU IDIOT! YOU INTER-FERING, MIND-LESS FOOL!

GIRI
(GRRK)

I... THOUGHT... YOU WERE...

I WAS... TRYING TO... STOP...

...A MURDEROUS PSYCHO-PATH HAS WALTZED OFF SCOT-FREE!

BECAUSE OF YOUR DAMNED MEDDLING...

HE HAS ES-CAPED!

ZUDA (SLAM)

AND YOU... YOU...

THIS WAS MY CHANCE TO STOP HIM...

...THAT I HAD MADE A TERRIBLE MISTAKE...

GUU (ZZZ)

GUU

I FINALLY REAL-IZED...

A MISTAKE THAT COULD NOT BE UNDONE...

A MISTAKE THAT COULD EVEN BE... FATAL.

CHAPTER 20:
VAMPIRES AND VAMPANEZE

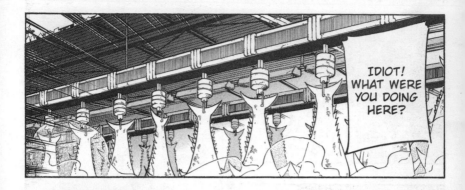

IDIOT! WHAT WERE YOU DOING HERE?

I THOUGHT YOU WERE THE KILLER.

I HEARD ABOUT THOSE SIX DEAD PEO-PLE ON THE NEWS...

KILL-ING HIM?!

TRYING TO STOP YOU...FROM KILLING HIM...

DO YOU TRULY HAVE SO LITTLE FAITH IN ME?!

YOU ARE EVEN DUMBER THAN I THOUGHT!

HOW CAN I TRUST YOU WHEN YOU WON'T TELL ME ANYTHING TO TRUST?!

YOU DISAPPEAR EVERY NIGHT, YOU NEVER TELL ME ANYTHING...

WHAT ELSE WAS I SUPPOSED TO THINK?

WHAT WAS I SUPPOSED TO THINK WHEN I HEARD SIX PEOPLE HAD BEEN FOUND DRAINED OF THEIR BLOOD?

HA
(GASP)

OF COURSE I'M GOING TO BE SUSPICIOUS!

YES. YOU ARE RIGHT.

I WISHED TO SPARE YOU THE GORY DETAILS. I SHOULD NOT HAVE.

THIS IS MY FAULT.

ONE MUST SHOW TRUST IN ORDER TO BE TRUSTED.

YOU MEANT TO KILL ME?

ER... YES...

I SHOULDN'T HAVE BEEN TRACKING YOU.

THAT'S OKAY... I GUESS I SHOULDN'T HAVE COME AFTER YOU LIKE I DID.

BUT I KNEW THAT WHEN I TOOK YOU ON AS MY ASSISTANT.

YOU ARE A RECKLESS YOUNG MAN, MASTER SHAN.

NIYA (SMIRK)

IN A WORST-CASE SCENARIO, I GUESS...

I WILL LIVE. A SHAME ABOUT MY COAT, HOW-EVER.

HA-HA.

WILL YOU BE OKAY?

I'M SORRY...

ZO (SHIVER)

WHO *WAS* HE...?

VAM-
PA-
NEZE?

HIS NAME IS MUR-LOUGH.

HE IS A VAMPA-NEZE.

LATER, I WILL ...

IT IS A LONG STORY. WE DO NOT HAVE TIME.

I WANT AN EX-PLANA-TION!

I CAN'T STAND BEING IN THE DARK ANYMORE!

I ALMOST KILLED YOU TONIGHT BECAUSE I DIDN'T KNOW WHAT WAS GOING ON!

NO! *NOT LATER, NOW!*

THE VAMPANEZE ...

...WHERE SHOULD I START?

NOW THEN ...

....

VERY WELL. I WILL NOT WITHHOLD SECRETS FROM YOU ANY LONGER.

IN OLDEN NIGHTS, HUMANS WERE LOOKED DOWN UPON BY MANY VAMPIRES ...

...WHO FED ON THEM AS PEOPLE FED ON ANIMALS.

IT WAS NOT UNUSUAL FOR VAMPIRES TO DRINK DRY A COUPLE OF PEOPLE A WEEK.

THERE-FORE, WE ESTABLISHED LAWS THAT FORBADE NEEDLESS KILLING.

AND EVEN VAMPIRES ORIGIN-ALLY CAME FROM HUMAN-ITY.

BUT WARS, PLAGUES AND FAMINE THREATENED TO WIPE OUT THE HUMAN POPULA-TION.

YES, THE VAMPANEZE. THEY CALLED THEMSELVES A SEPARATE RACE AND ESTABLISHED THEIR OWN RULES AND GOVERNING BODIES.

AND THOSE WERE ...

THEY THOUGHT OUR NATURAL WAY HAD BEEN STOLEN FROM US.

MOST VAMPIRES WERE CONTENT TO OBEY THE LAWS, BUT SOME WERE NOT.

SEVEN HUNDRED YEARS AGO, EVENTS CAME TO A HEAD. SEVENTY VAMPIRES BROKE AWAY AND DECLARED INDEPENDENCE.

BASICALLY, THE VAMPANEZE BELIEVE THERE IS SHAME IN TAKING SMALL AMOUNTS OF BLOOD FROM A HUMAN AT A TIME.

THEY BELIEVE THERE IS NOBILITY IN DRAINING A PERSON AND ABSORBING THEIR SPIRIT...

...AS YOU ABSORBED PART OF SAM GREST'S.

...TO WAGE A LONG, LONG WAR AGAINST EACH OTHER.

IT IS THAT VERY DIS-AGREEMENT WHICH LED VAMPIRE AND VAM-PANEZE...

COR-RECT.

SO THEY ALWAYS KILL THE PEOPLE THEY DRINK FROM?

THAT'S TERRIBLE! WHY CAN'T THEY JUST TAKE ENOUGH TO SURVIVE?

THE VAMPIRES WERE WINNING, HOWEVER. WE WOULD HAVE HUNTED THE VAMPANEZE OUT OF EXISTENCE...

...IF WE HAD NOT BEEN STOPPED.

...AND MUCH BLOOD WAS SHED ON BOTH SIDES.

THE FIGHTING WAS TERRIBLE...

W-WHAT DO YOU MEAN?

THE VERY HUMANS WE WERE TRYING TO PROTECT...

...GOT IN THE WAY.

THE HUMANS COULD NOT TELL THE DIFFERENCE BETWEEN VAMPIRES AND VAMPANEZE.

KUKU (CHEH HEH)

NIYARI (SMRK)

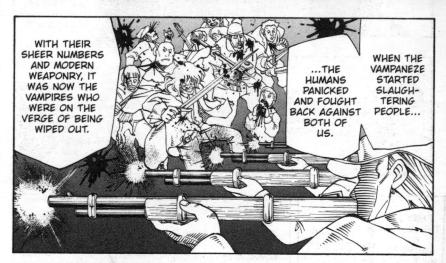

WITH THEIR SHEER NUMBERS AND MODERN WEAPONRY, IT WAS NOW THE VAMPIRES WHO WERE ON THE VERGE OF BEING WIPED OUT.

...THE HUMANS PANICKED AND FOUGHT BACK AGAINST BOTH OF US.

WHEN THE VAMPANEZE STARTED SLAUGHTERING PEOPLE...

...AND A TRUCE WAS AGREED TO.

IN THE END, OUR PRINCES MET WITH THE VAMPANEZE...

...SO THAT THE VAMPIRES AND VAMPANEZE WOULD NOT CLASH AND WAR ANY LONGER.

WE AGREED TO LIVE APART FROM ONE ANOTHER...

WE WOULD LEAVE THEM ALONE IF THEY STOPPED MURDERING SO FREELY.

LIKE MURLOUGH?

TIME HAS CHANGED THE VAMPANEZE AND THEIR APPEARANCE.

FOR CENTURIES WE HAVE MAINTAINED THIS SEPARATION.

MOST VAMPANEZE ARE NOT AS COLOURFUL AS MURLOUGH.

THEY'RE THE REASON WHY VAMPIRES HAVE SUCH A BAD REPUTATION!

SO THE VAMPANEZE ARE EVIL.

AFTER SEVERAL DECADES, YOUNG VAMPANEZE WILL FIND THEIR SKIN CHANGING TO THAT HORRID COLOUR.

PURPLE SKIN, RED EYES.

THESE CHANGES CAME ABOUT BECAUSE THEY DRINK MORE BLOOD THAN VAMPIRES.

GU (GULP)

IT IS HOW SOLDIERS WHO MURDER OTHERS IN BATTLE COME TO BE CALLED HEROES.

GOOD AND EVIL CHANGE ACCORDING TO THE TIME, SITUATION, AND OBSERVER, DARREN.

TO US, THEY ARE MORE LIKE MISGUIDED COUSINS.

THAT IS NOT ENTIRELY TRUE.

THE VAMPANEZE ARE ONLY KILLING ACCORDING TO THEIR BELIEFS AND LAWS.

I WAS GOING TO EXECUTE HIM.

WHAT WERE YOU GOING TO DO WITH MURLOUGH, THEN?

HE IS STARVING FOR BLOOD.

HE HAS LOST CONTROL AND KILLS INDISCRIMINATELY, FEEDING HIS LUNATIC LUST.

MADNESS HAS INVADED MURLOUGH'S MIND.

HUH...?

グ グーゴー
ゴー

GUGOO (SNORR)

GUGOO

LOOK AT THE LEFT CHEEK OF THIS MAN.

VAMPANEZE SELECT THEIR VICTIMS IN ADVANCE, AND PUT THREE SMALL SCRATCHES ON THE LEFT CHEEK.

IT IS THE MARK OF THEIR PREY.

LOOK CLOSER.

η"ゔ" GUGO...

I DON'T SEE ANY-THING...

OH!

NOT ONLY THAT, HE IS CRAFTIER THAN MOST.

MURLOUGH MAY BE MAD, BUT HE STILL HOLDS TO THE VAMPANEZE LAWS.

I ONLY HAD TO SIT BACK AND WAIT FOR MURLOUGH ...

...SO I CONTINUED TRACKING HIM.

I WAS LUCKY ENOUGH TO SPOT THE MARKED MAN...

...BUT INSTEAD, *YOU* ARRIVED ON THE SCENE.

ISN'T THAT EVEN *MORE* REASON WHY YOU SHOULD GO AFTER HIM?!

MURLOUGH IS NO FOOL. HE WILL BE LEAVING THIS CITY AS WE SPEAK.

!?

I SUPPOSE I WILL HAVE TO SETTLE ON THIS, AFTER ALL MY HARD WORK.

AREN'T YOU GOING TO FOLLOW HIM?!

YES. THE ONLY THING THAT MATTERS TO ME IS THAT HE HAS LEFT *THIS* CITY.

YOU'RE JUST GOING TO LET HIM TERRORIZE ANOTHER CITY?

IT IS NOT MY PLACE TO WORRY ABOUT CREATURES SUCH AS HIM.

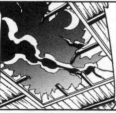

...IT IS SIMPLY AN ISSUE OF MY OWN RESPONSIBILITY.

IF A SINGLE VAMPIRE SUCH AS MYSELF KILLS A VAMPANEZE...

THEN WHY ARE *YOU* GETTING INVOLVED?

IT WOULD BREAK THE PEACE ACCORD IF THEY INTERVENED.

AT WORST, IT COULD SPARK ALL-OUT WAR.

THE HANDS OF THE VAMPIRE GENERALS ARE TIED IN MATTERS SUCH AS THESE.

MY LIFE IS A TRIFLING PRICE TO PAY FOR PROTECTING THIS CITY AND AVERTING A WAR.

THEY WILL CHASE YOU TO THE ENDS OF THE EARTH TO AVENGE THE MURDER OF ONE OF THEIR OWN.

THE VAMPANEZE ARE A LOYAL SORT.

WHY WOULD YOU GET SO INVOLVED WITH THIS PLACE ...?

BECAUSE THIS IS THE CITY WHERE I WAS BORN.

GAVNER FOUND ME IN ORDER TO TELL ME THIS BIT OF NEWS, KNOWING THAT I WOULD BE FORCED INTO ACTION.

KU (HEH) KU...

...THIS, MORE THAN ANY OTHER PLACE, IS WHAT I CONSIDER HOME.

I LIVED HERE AS A HUMAN.

THOUGH EVERYONE I KNEW THEN HAS LONG SINCE DIED...

S-SO NOW THAT YOUR CITY IS SAFE, YOU DON'T CARE ABOUT MURLOUGH ANYMORE?

...I DO NOT THINK IT PRESSING THAT WE RETURN TO THE CIRQUE DU FREAK IMMEDIATELY.

I KNOW IT SEEMS HARSH, BUT THIS IS THE VAMPIRE WAY. WE CAN DO NO MORE.

I COULD HEAR YOU EVERY DAY, CARRYING ON ABOUT CHRISTMAS THIS, AND CHRISTMAS THAT.

I AM NOT AGAINST SPENDING CHRISTMAS HERE...

HA-HA, SORRY. I'M SURE EVRA WILL—

YOU DISTURBED MY SLEEP WITH ALL THAT SHOUTING.

BIKU (TWITCH)

SNRRT!

OH, NO! *EVRA!!*

I FORGOT!

YOU LITTLE RASCALS.

THE SNAKE-BOY KNEW ABOUT THIS TOO?

SURE THING.

HURRY AND GET HIM. YOU WILL HAVE TO EXPLAIN THE TRUTH.

GAGAGAGA... (CREEEAK)

LET US GO. HE WILL WAKE SOON.

UNGH...

UHH...

IT'S SAFE TO COME OUT, NOW...

EVRA...

EVRAAAA!

SHIIINT
(SHHHH)

BARI
(CRINK)

MR. CREPSLEY WASN'T THE KILLER. I WAS ...

EVRA, IT'S ALL OKAY.

THAT'S STRANGE ...

TRRR

VVVV
VVV...

... EVRA
?!

E-

KOKU
(NOD)

... EVRA'S
?

H-HIS
PHONE...

WHAT
IS
IT?

DO YOU ...THINK MURLOUGH GOT HIM?

NOT GOOD.

THIS IS MURLOUGH'S SCENT.

KUN (SNIFF)

...THEN EVRA IS DEAD.

IF SO...

EVRA... NO!!!

CHAPTER 21:
THE EVIL BENEATH

EVRA... WHERE ARE YOU NOW?

SO I RAN TO CATCH UP!

I SAW YOU WALKING OUTSIDE FROM MY WINDOW.

HAA

HAA (HUFF)

DARREN!!

TATA (TEK TEK)

NOPE. NO CRYING...

HAVE YOU BEEN CRY-ING?

YOUR FACE LOOKS WHITE AS A SHEET, AND YOUR EYES...

I DON'T KNOW...

B-BUT YOU SAID THEY WOULD...

YOUR DAD AND YOUR BROTHER EVRA ARE COMING OVER...

...AREN'T THEY?

....

ARE YOU READY FOR CHRISTMAS EVE TOMORROW?

SORRY, DEBBIE! I JUST REMEMBERED SOMETHING I'VE REALLY GOT TO TAKE CARE OF!

HEY, DARREN!

GOOO (WHSHHH)

DON'T FORGET ABOUT TOMORROW!

WE'LL BE WAITING FOR YOU!

JARI...
(SCRAPE)

...LIKE
EVRA...

I'M
SORRY,
DEBBIE.
THERE
ARE MORE
IMPORTANT
THINGS ON
MY MIND
...

HEY.
DARREN
SHAN.

MUCH
TASTIER-
LOOKING
THAN YOUR
OTHER FRIEND,
THE SNAKE-
BOY, HMMM?

I LIKE
YOUR
GIRL-
FRIEND.
A VERY
TASTY
DISH...

DO YOU
THINK SHE
LIKES
PURPLE?

HEH
HEH
HEH
...

MURLOUGH?!

GOGA
(CLUNKS)

ARGH!!

HYU
(ZIP)

BAGAN
(THWUP)

ANY CLOSER, AND THAT'LL BE THE END OF SNAKEY...

BACK, BOY, BACK.

CHI-CHI (TSK)

MUR-LOUGH!!

YOUNG MURLOUGH MAKES A GREAT CONDUCTOR!

HE SCREAMS SO LOUD!

EVERY TIME I PULL ONE OFF, "DARREN! DARREN!"

SNAKEY'S SCALES!

OF COURSE. YOUNG MURLOUGH'S GOT PLENTY OF PATIENCE, YES HE HAS.

THERE WILL BE NO EASY DEATH FOR SNAKEY.

THAT MEANS HE'S STILL ALIVE, THEN!

PORON (FLIK)

PORON

DO YOU RECOGNIZE THIS?

AND THEN HE'S DEAD...

HEE-HEE-HEE!

BUT ONLY UNTIL CHRISTMAS.

VAMPANEZE DO NOT LIE.

IF I SAY HE'S ALIVE, HE'S ALIVE.

P-PROVE TO ME THAT HE'S ALIVE.

THAT FOOLISH, MEDDLING VAMPIRE!!

GO (GRONK)

YOU AND YOUR MASTER RUINED MY GLORIOUS PLANS!

BUT I *WANTED* TO DRAIN THE *FAT MAN*...

GIRI GIRI (GRIT)

YOU MEAN MR. CREPS-LEY?

WHAT HAPPENED TO THE **OTHER** VAMPIRE ...?

I'VE BEEN PLAYING, DARREN SHAN.

FUUU

FUUU (CHFFF)

LARTEN CREPS-LEY, YES?

AHH, YES ...

THAT WAS **CREPS-LEY...**

WHAT SORT OF A DEAL?

...BUT I THINK WE CAN MAKE A DEAL, CAN'T WE?

YOU LOOK LIKE A SMART BOY. NOT AS SMART AS YOUNG MURLOUGH...

WHY NOT THAT ?!

I'LL GIVE YOU **ME** FOR EVRA!

I'LL DO NO SUCH THING!

IF YOU WANT SNAKEY BACK...

...YOU HAND OVER CREPS-LEY.

A VERY SIMPLE SWAP.

I WANT TO RIP HIM TO SHREDS!

MURLOUGH WANTS CREPSLEY, YES HE DOES!

GU (HRG)

VAMPANEZE CANNOT DRINK THE BLOOD OF VAMPIRES ANYWAY!

YOUR LITTLE HALF-VAMPIRE BLOOD IS USELESS TO ME!

I DON'T CARE ABOUT YOU!

BRING CREPSLEY TO ME, NOW!!

THAT INSANE VAMPIRE BROKE OUR LAWS!

NITAA (GRIN)

YOU'LL GET ME FOR EVRA, OR NOTHING AT ALL!

I'LL NEVER DO THAT...

!!

THEN I'LL KILL YOU IN-STEAD!

ZUSHA
(ZSHHK)

BUN
(VOOM)

YOU WOULDN'T DARE!!

I'LL EAT YOUR TASTY LITTLE GIRL-FRIEND TOO.

I'LL KILL YOU LATER, ALONG WITH SNAKEY AND CREPSLEY...

HEE HEE HEE... BUT NOT YET!

JI...

JIJI JI (PRIP, PIP)

IT WILL BE A VERY GOOD CHRIST-MAS FEAST...

JUST WAIT AND SEE, HMMM?

SFX: NUYA... (SLURP)

9

WON'T IT, DARREN SHAN?!

IHI (CHWA)

UHYA (WAH)

HYA (CHA)

HYA

YES, THE GREATEST CHRISTMAS EVER!

HYA

HYA

HYA

MUR-LOUGH! THAT RAT. I DID NOT THINK HE WOULD STILL BE HERE...

YOU KNOW I COULDN'T DO THAT.

WE COULD HAVE LAID A TRAP...

IT IS UNFORTUNATE THAT YOU REFUSED TO SWAP ME FOR EVRA, HOWEVER.

BUT WHY? YOU MUST PREFER EVRA TO ME.

YES, BUT WE SAID WE'D TRUST EACH OTHER, REMEMBER?

I HAVE GRAVELY UNDER-ESTIMATED YOU, DARREN.

AHEM!

KOFF!!

I FEEL HONOURED TO HAVE YOU BY MY SIDE...

THE VAM-PANEZE ARE TRUE TO THEIR WORD.

UNLESS MUR-LOUGH CHANGES HIS MIND.

THERE IS STILL HOPE. IT IS NOW THE TWENTY-THIRD, AND WE HAVE UNTIL CHRISTMAS MORNING TO SAVE HIM.

...SO, WHAT ABOUT EVRA?

...I WILL TRADE *MY* LIFE FOR HIS.

AND IF WE SHOULD RUN INTO MURLOUGH BEFORE WE CAN RESCUE EVRA...

AND THEN WE BEGAN A SEARCH FOR HIS HIDEOUT...

...SO THAT MURLOUGH COULDN'T SEE US FROM THE SEWERS.

WE SWITCHED TO A NEW HOTEL, MOVING ACROSS THE ROOF-TOPS...

HOTEL THE PAOLO

...OR MUR-LOUGH WILL SPOT US SOONER.

DO NOT USE THE TORCH UNLESS THERE IS ABSOLUTELY NO LIGHT TO SEE BY...

DOWN HERE, HE CAN MOVE FREELY, WITH NO FEAR OF SUNLIGHT OR PRYING EYES.

AHA. CLEVER MOVE, MUR-LOUGH.

ZAZAZA...
(FSHHHH)

NOW, LET US BE OFF.

KOKU
(NOD)
コクッ

CHICHI...
(TWIT
TWIT)

チチ
チチ...

CHICHI...

WE WILL NOT BE ABLE TO FIND HIM, EVEN IF WE SEARCHED WITHOUT REST.

I AM AFRAID WE MUST FALL BACK.

IT IS LARGER AND MORE COMPLEX DOWN HERE THAN I HAD IMAGINED.

BLAST THESE INFERNAL SEWERS! THE NIGHT IS ALREADY OVER.

IS THAT CLEAR?

WE SHOULD RETURN AND FORM A PLAN.

WE WILL FIND NOTHING BY BLINDLY GROPING ABOUT.

NO! LET'S SEARCH MORE!

CALM DOWN, DARREN!

BAN (WHAM)

ONLY A DAY AND A HALF LEFT... WE JUST DON'T HAVE TIME!!

HOTEL THE PACLO

LOOK WHAT'S HAPPENED TO EVERY SINGLE FRIEND I'VE EVER HAD...

WHY AM I... SO HELP-LESS?

DAMMIT! DAMMIT!!

PICKLED ONIONS

124

AND I DID NOTHING...

KORO
(ROLL)

DARREN.

GIVE ME YOUR STRENGTH, SAM...

HELP ME SAVE EVRA, SAM!

GYU
(GRPP)

SAM!!

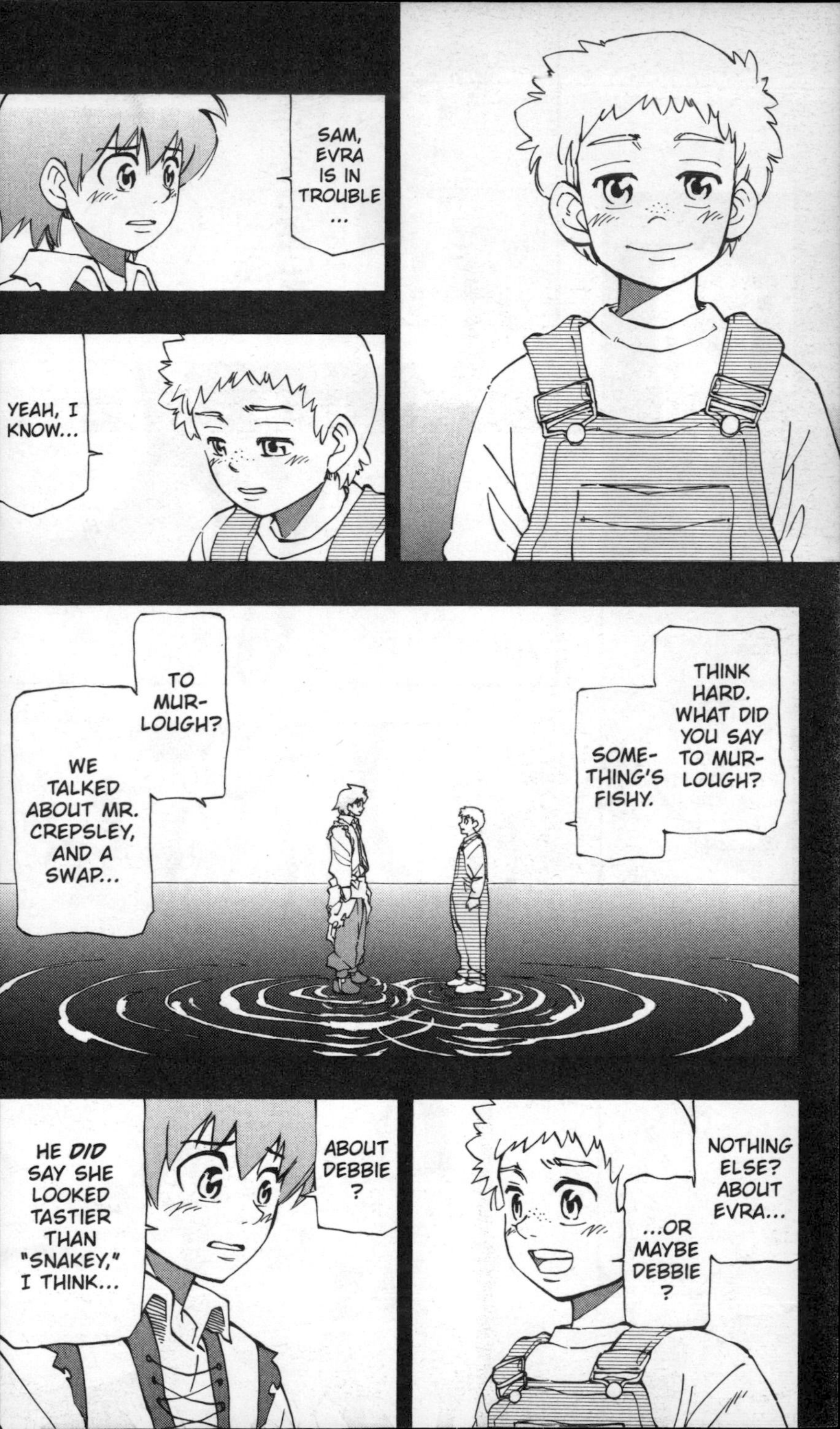
SAM, EVRA IS IN TROUBLE ...
YEAH, I KNOW...
THINK HARD. WHAT DID YOU SAY TO MUR-LOUGH?
SOME-THING'S FISHY.
TO MUR-LOUGH?
WE TALKED ABOUT MR. CREPSLEY, AND A SWAP...
HE *DID* SAY SHE LOOKED TASTIER THAN "SNAKEY," I THINK...
ABOUT DEBBIE ?
NOTHING ELSE? ABOUT EVRA...
...OR MAYBE DEBBIE ?

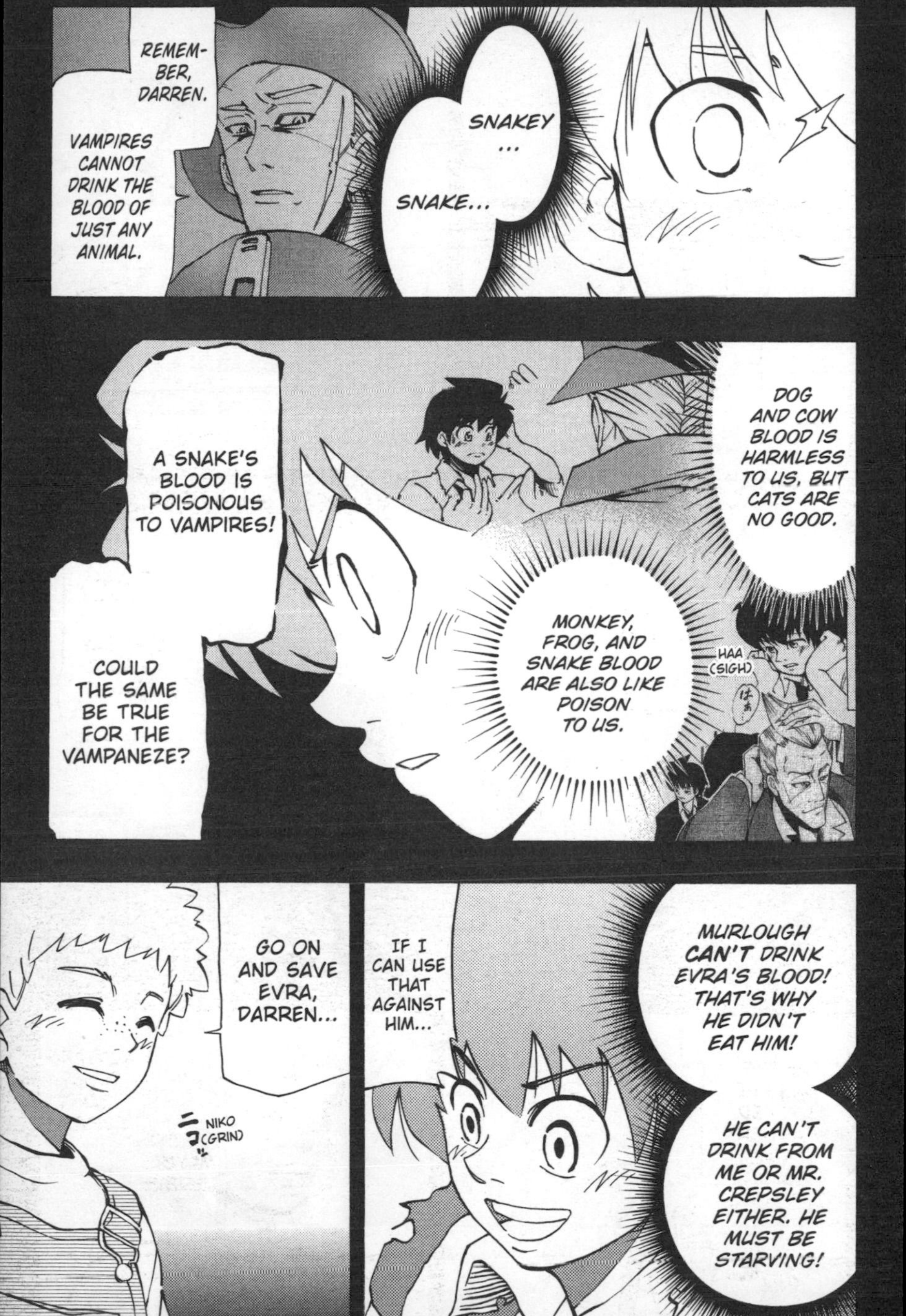

REMEMBER, DARREN.
VAMPIRES CANNOT DRINK THE BLOOD OF JUST ANY ANIMAL.
SNAKEY ...
SNAKE...
A SNAKE'S BLOOD IS POISONOUS TO VAMPIRES!
DOG AND COW BLOOD IS HARMLESS TO US, BUT CATS ARE NO GOOD.
MONKEY, FROG, AND SNAKE BLOOD ARE ALSO LIKE POISON TO US.
HAA (SIGH)
COULD THE SAME BE TRUE FOR THE VAMPANEZE?
GO ON AND SAVE EVRA, DARREN...
NIKO (GRIN)
IF I CAN USE THAT AGAINST HIM...
MURLOUGH CAN'T DRINK EVRA'S BLOOD! THAT'S WHY HE DIDN'T EAT HIM!
HE CAN'T DRINK FROM ME OR MR. CREPSLEY EITHER. HE MUST BE STARVING!

THANKS, SAM...

MR. CREPSLEY...

WE MIGHT BE ABLE TO SAVE EVRA AFTER ALL...

I THINK I HAVE A PLAN.

CHAPTER 22:
THE ROAD TO EVRA

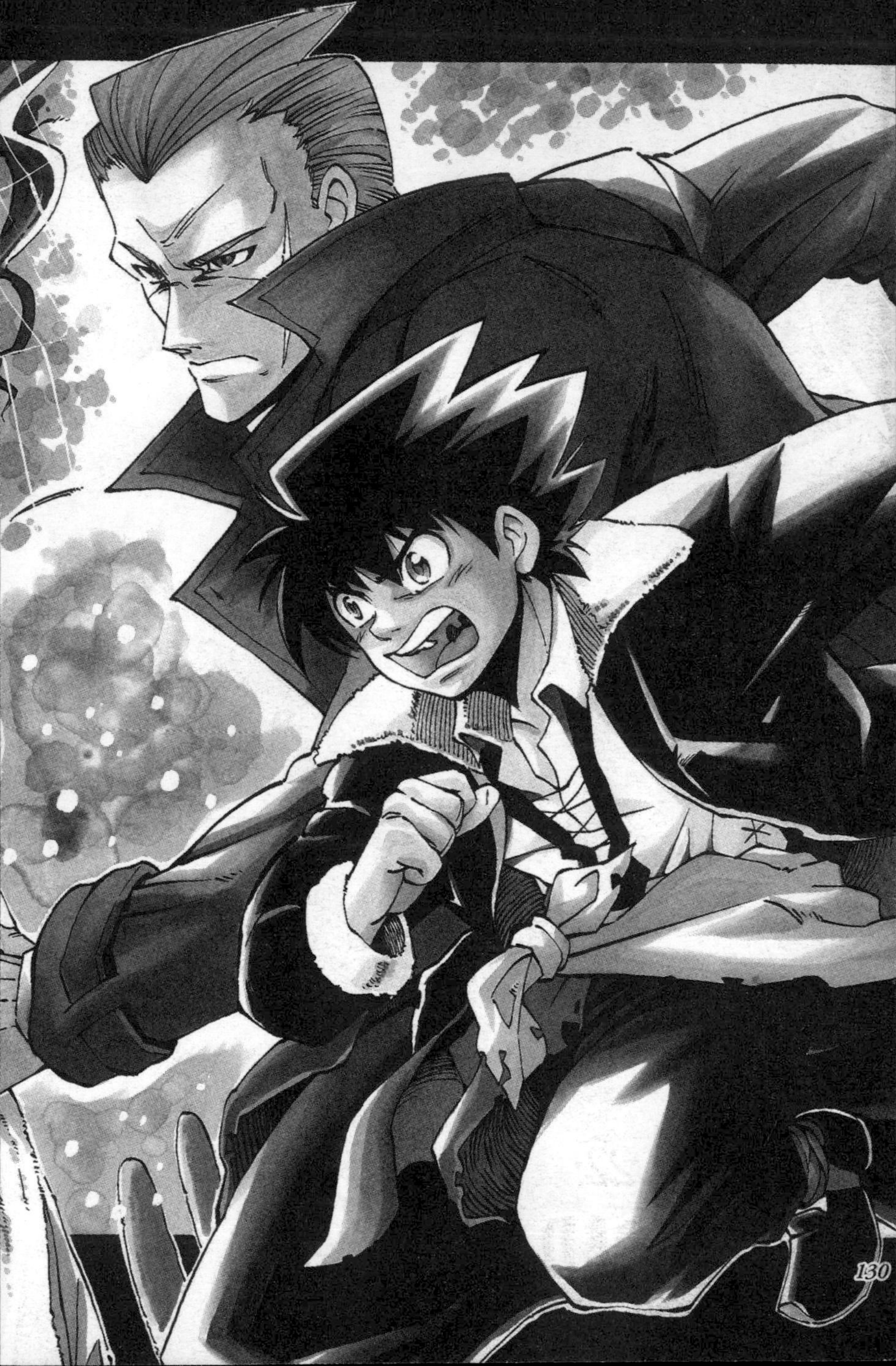

CHAPTER 22:
THE ROAD TO EVRA

10:00 A.M., DECEMBER 24TH—CHRISTMAS EVE.

HELLO, DEBBIE?

...Darren?

SORRY ABOUT YESTERDAY. SAY, IS IT ALL RIGHT IF I COME OVER TODAY AFTER ALL?

You'll come?! Please do! Mum's cooking the dinner already.

NO, JUST ME.

Oh. That's too bad...

Will your brother and dad be there too?

THANKS, DEBBIE. SEE YOU THERE.

I'm glad you're coming, though!

FUU (SIGH)

GACHA (CLICK)

PATAN
(THUMP)

PIN-PONN
(DING-DONG)

CHU

CHU
(SMEK)

OH, DARREN! MERRY CHRISTMAS!

YOU SURPRISED ME! WHY DIDN'T YOU USE THE FRONT DOOR?

UMMM...

THINK QUICK!

DEBBIE! THERE'S A HANDSOME PIRATE HERE TO SEE YOU!

MY DAD GAVE THIS TO ME TO BRING OVER.

AS IF ANYONE CARES ABOUT CARPETS AT CHRISTMAS.

OH, YOU SILLY BOY.

MY SHOES ARE WET FROM THE DIRTY SLUSH.

I DIDN'T WANT TO DIRTY YOUR CARPETS.

THIS IS BETTER THAN THE WINE WE BOUGHT!

WELL, WELL!

STOP IT, DAD!

RIGHT, DEBBIE?

WE INVITED THE RIGHT MAN OVER. WE SHOULD HAVE HIM AROUND MORE OFTEN!

I HAVE TO LEAVE BEFORE EVENING.

UH, ABOUT THAT...

THANKS FOR COMING, DARREN!

WE'RE GOING TO HAVE A GREAT TIME TONIGHT!

WHAT? WHY?

WE'RE ACTUALLY LEAVING TOWN TONIGHT TO GO AND SEE MY MUM.

ALL THREE OF US...

SO THIS IS YOUR LAST AFTERNOON TOGETHER...

NOW YOU GET TO SPEND CHRISTMAS WITH YOUR FAMILY.

......

T-THAT'S GREAT! I BET IT'S THE BEST PRESENT YOU COULD HAVE HOPED FOR!

DA-A-A-AD!!

ALAS! FATE HAS DRIVEN THE YOUNG ROMANTICS APART!

RIGHT, DARREN?

IT'S OUR JOB TO EMBAR-RASS OUR DAUGHTERS IN FRONT OF BOY-FRIENDS.

THAT'S WHAT FATHERS ARE FOR.

DON'T SAY THAT! IT'S EMBAR-RASSING!

HA-HA...

UH, YEAH...

AHA! FINALLY!

DINNER'S READY!

EVERY-ONE TO THE TABLE!

HA HA HA!

OH, YOU!

I COULD EVEN EAT THE CUTLERY.

THIS MEAL IS SO GOOD!

NO, I'LL DO IT. YOU'VE BEEN SERVING ALL AFTERNOON.

GATA (THUMP)

I'LL GO AND GET THE BOTTLE ...

I CERTAINLY AM!

I THINK IT MIGHT BE TIME FOR THAT WINE NOW. ARE WE READY?

THAT'S IT! NO PRESENTS FOR *YOU* TOMORROW!

I THINK I'LL EXCHANGE DEBBIE FOR DARREN. HE'S *MUCH* MORE USEFUL TO HAVE AROUND.

PON
(POP)

SMELLS
NICE...

YOU
OKAY IN
HERE?

DAR-
REN
...

Y-
YEAH,
OF
COURSE
...

BESIDES,
IT'S NOT
LIKE WE
CAN NEVER
SEE EACH
OTHER
AGAIN.

I'M
JUST
KID-
DING.

SORRY.
IT WAS
ALL SO
SUDDEN
...

I WISH I
COULD HAVE
DECORATED
THE TREE
WITH YOU.

I'M GLAD TO SEE THAT...

YOU LOOK BETTER TODAY, THOUGH.

YOU SEEMED SO TENSE AND PREOCCUPIED...

I WAS WORRIED YESTERDAY.

KYU (SQUEEZE)

W-WHAT'S WRONG, DEBBIE?

AM I NOT ALLOWED TO HUG YOU WITHOUT A REASON?

140

JUST AN EARLY CHRISTMAS PRESENT.

WHAT'S THIS?

DAD'S DYING FOR THAT WINE.

OH, AND HURRY UP.

DON'T WORRY, IT'S ONLY A TOY RING.

BUT I DON'T HAVE ANYTHING FOR YOU ...

TOKU (DOOK)

TOKU

POTA (PLIP)

GOSO (RUSTLE)

AND NOW, A TOAST ...

AHEM ...

WHAT TOOK YOU SO LONG? WE WERE ABOUT TO SEND A SEARCH PARTY TO LOOK FOR YOU!

AND HERE IT IS!

CHEERS!

CHEERS!

TO THE HEMLOCKS, AND THEIR YOUNG LOVERS!

CHEERS!

CHIN (TING)

GOKU (GULP)

GUI (SIP)

JARI
(SCRAPE)

YEAH,
KIND
OF...

WAS
DINNER
WITH
YOUR
GIRL-
FRIEND
ENJOY-
ABLE?

GYU
(SQUEEZE)

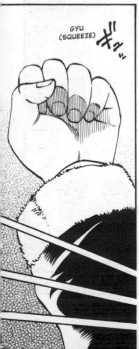

THEN
LET US
RESUME
OUR SEARCH
FOR EVRA.

HEH
...

BASA
(FLAP)

HAA

HAA (HUFF)

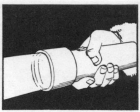

I DON'T CARE HOW MUCH NOISE WE MAKE!

TO HELL WITH BEING CAREFUL! THIS IS OUR LAST CHANCE TO FIND HIM!

WE MUST BE MORE CARE-FUL!

SLOW DOWN! HE WILL HEAR US IF YOU KEEP THIS UP.

GIVE IT TO ME!!

STOP IT! BEHAVE YOUR-SELF!

BASHI (THWAP)

MINE'S OUT OF BATTERIES.

GIVE ME THAT TORCH!

YOU DON'T CARE ABOUT EVRA, DO YOU?!

YOU MUST CALM DOWN! I UNDER-STAND THAT YOU ARE—

AAAH!!!

GASHAA
CCRSHHD

I'LL SAVE EVRA BY MY- SELF!

I'M GOING ON MY OWN!

SHUT UP! GO AND GET A NEW ONE, THEN!

I TOLD YOU THIS WOULD HAPPEN!

YOU IDIOT! NOW WE WILL HAVE TO GO BACK UP AND FIND A REPLACE- MENT!

YOU CANNOT! NOT ALONE!

COME BACK, DAR- REN!!

EVRAAAAAA!!

STOP! MUR- LOUGH WILL HEAR! DARREN!

HAA
(CHUFF)

HAA

BASHA
(SPLASH)

BASHA

I'M COMING TO FIND YOU! YELL IF YOU CAN HEAR ME!

EVRA! IT'S ME! DAR-REN!

I CAN'T HEAR HIS VOICE ANY-MORE.

WE'RE COM-PLETELY SEPA-RATED NOW.

DO
(WHAM)

E
V
R
A
A
A
A
A
A
!!

DA
(DSHH)

AAAH!

BASHA

M
U
R
L
O
U
G
H
...

M-

DID YOU
FOLLOW
ME
DOWN?

W-
WHO'S
THERE?
IS THAT
YOU, MR.
CREPS-
LEY?

DON'T YOU
RECOGNIZE
THESE
FANGS?

HEH-HEH-
HEH...
SORRY,
BUT NO.

NITAA
(GREEE)

GEHO
(COFF)

GEHO

DAMN!
SLEEPING
GAS!

GURAA
(LRCH)

PICHAN
(DRIP)

PICHAN

MUR-
LOUGH
...

BASHA
(SPLSH)

UH...

NNG
...

ARE YOU AWAKE, DARREN SHAN?

BATA (THWUP)

BATA

SAY HELLO TO EVRA.

SU (SHH)

GI (GRRK)

PICHA (DRIP)

WHY ARE THE DRIPS SOUNDING FROM ABOVE?

"HELLO, DARREN!"
AAAAAHH!!
JUKU
JUKU
(SKITTLE)

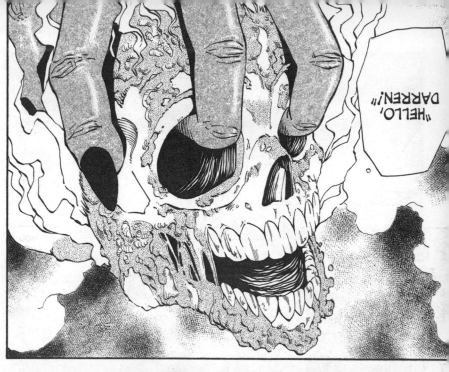

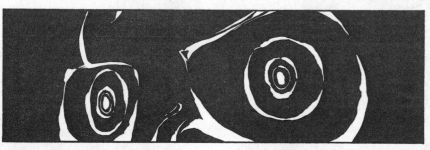

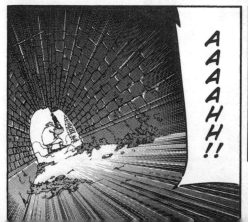

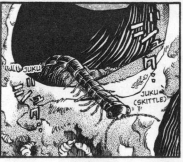

CHAPTER 23:
HELD CAPTIVE

I THOUGHT VAMPANEZE NEVER WENT BACK ON THEIR WORD!

YOU PROM-ISED YOU WOULDN'T KILL HIM BEFORE CHRIST-MAS!

GACHA (GREK)

GICHI (GREK)

HI (CHEE)

HI

HI

D-D-D... DAR-REN?

WHAT ARE YOU DOING HERE, DARREN?

PASHI

PASHI (TOSS)

YOU WILL BE HOSTAGES TO LURE CREPSLEY HERE...SO I CAN *KILL HIM!*

I'M SO GLAD YOU'RE STILL ALIVE, EVRA...

ANY FUNNY BUSINESS FROM YOU, AND I'LL CARVE YOU UP LIKE ROAST TURKEY.

TOO EARLY FOR RELIEF, THOUGH. YOUNG MURLOUGH IS HUNGRY... AND *ANGRY.*

YOU DIDN'T NEED ME. YOU COULD HAVE TAKEN HIM OUT IN THE DARK- NESS...

WHY DIDN'T YOU KILL HIM EARLIER, THEN?

CREPSLEY STOLE MY CHRISTMAS FEAST, AND EVEN TRIED TO KILL *ME* TOO!

HE MUST *PAY* FOR HIS CRIMES!

KAN (CLAK)

...BUT PERHAPS YOU ARE RIGHT. MAYBE I NEEDN'T HAVE DONE THIS.

POI (TOSS)

HE IS A WILY, OLD VAMPIRE. I WANT TO BE 100% ASSURED OF VICTORY...

IT'S A MATTER OF ODDS, DARREN SHAN.

GOSHA (CRUNCH)

HE WANDERED BLINDLY INTO MY TERRITORY AND GOT HIS APPRENTICE KIDNAPPED!

HOW FOOLISH CAN YOU BE?!

WHO CARES ABOUT THE EX-AGGERATIONS OF A BATTLE-HARDENED, "LEGENDARY" VAMPIRE?

YOU CAN'T DRINK FROM ME. I'M A VAMPIRE AND YOU'RE A VAM-PANEZE.

YOU EVEN SAID IT YOUR-SELF.

MANY TIMES SMARTER THAN HIS MASTER...

A GOOD MEMORY HE HAS.

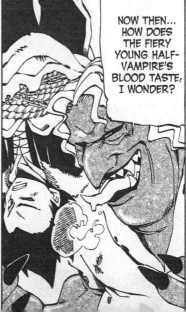

NOW THEN... HOW DOES THE FIERY YOUNG HALF-VAMPIRE'S BLOOD TASTE, I WONDER?

GIRI
(GRIT)

UNLESS YOU AL-READY *TRIED?*

WHY DON'T YOU TRY IT? ASSUMING VAMPANEZE CAN ACTUALLY DRINK SNAKE'S BLOOD.

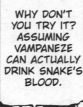

WHAT ABOUT SNAKEY'S BLOOD, THOUGH?

I TOOK A LITTLE SIP FROM HIM AND THREW UP FOR HOURS AFTER!

YOU'RE RIGHT, I DID!

DAMN IT ALL, DAMN! YOU LITTLE WRETCHES HAVE DESTROYED MY PLANS FOR A FEAST!

INSTEAD OF A JUICY FAT MAN, I'LL HAVE TO FEED ON RATS!

THAT'S NOT HOW IT WORKS!

WHY WERE YOU SO FIXATED ON THE FAT MAN?

THERE ARE PLENTY OF HUMANS UP ABOVE US...

I WANTED TASTY BLOOD...A FEAST FOR CHRISTMAS...

GAKU
(SLUMP)

WHAT A TER-RIBLE CHRIST-MAS THIS IS...

NOW I NO LONGER HAVE THAT TIME!

THAT'S WHY WE MAKE PLANS AND MARK OUR PREY AHEAD OF TIME!

WE'RE NOT STUPID ENOUGH TO DRINK AT RANDOM!

VAMPANEZE HAVE SO MUCH MORE BRAINS IN THEIR HEADS THAN VAMPIRES!

DON'T GET HIM ANY ANGRIER THAN HE ALREADY IS.

STOP IT, DAR-REN...

AND ONCE I'M DONE WITH HIM, IT WILL BE *YOUR* TURN NEXT!

BLAST THAT ACCURSED CREPSLEY! I WILL KILL HIM! I WILL FLAY THE SKIN FROM HIS BONES!

GASHA

GASHA (STOMP)

DON'T WORRY... WE'LL GET OUT OF THIS ONE. MR. CREPSLEY WILL DO SOMETHING...

...DAR-REN?

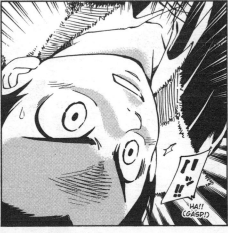

HA!! (GASP!)

... MR. CREPS-LEY WILL ...

PIKU (TWIK)

...HA-HA, OF COURSE!

SO *THAT'S* WHAT IT IS!

WAIT A MINUTE. I HAVE TO THINK SOME-THING THROUGH.

WHAT IS IT?

WHAT WERE YOU GOING TO SAY?

WHAT IS IT?

I NEVER CONSID-ERED THAT HE MIGHT...

イラ
イラ
イラ
IRA (HRG)
IRA

YOU'RE GOING TO HAVE TO LEAVE HERE IF YOU KILL ME, AREN'T YOU?

I HAVEN'T GOT ALL NIGHT, DARREN SHAN!

SPEAK WHILE YOU'RE ABLE!!

GIN (SHLING)

PLENTY!

WHAT DOES YOUR DEATH HAVE TO DO WITH THIS CITY?!

LEAVE?!

GASHA (CLANK)

THIS CAVERN IS THE HEART, WHERE THE BLOOD OF THE CITY FLOWS IN AND OUT.

THESE TUNNELS ARE LIKE VEINS.

YOU KNOW WHAT BEING DOWN HERE MAKES ME FEEL LIKE? AS IF I'M IN THE BODY OF THE CITY!

YOU THINK I WILL LEAVE MY BEAUTIFUL TUNNELS? NEVER!

IT IS A PARA- DISE.

IMAGINE LIVING IN A BODY, ROAMING THE VEINS...

AND WHY HAVEN'T YOU TOLD ME THE *REASON* YET?!

...BECAUSE YOU *WILL* HAVE TO LEAVE.

THAT'S REALLY TOO BAD...

IT *WAS* FOOLISH, YOU'RE RIGHT. MR. CREPSLEY IS SMARTER THAN THAT...

WE WERE RUNNING AROUND IN YOUR TERRITORY, SHOUTING AND WAVING TORCHES.

WE'VE BEEN *USED*, EVRA... BY MR. CREPSLEY.

I FINALLY FIGURED IT OUT.

BUT THERE ARE EXCEP- TIONS.

THE PACT BETWEEN VAMPIRES AND VAMPANEZE PREVENTS THEM FROM INTERFERING WITH ONE ANOTHER.

I'M REMINDED OF SOME- THING HE TOLD ME.

IF YOU KILL ME, MR. CREPSLEY WILL BRING THE GENERALS TO DESTROY YOU.

WHAT'S YOUR POINT?!

ISN'T THAT RIGHT?

IN THE CASE OF MURDER, IT IS ACCEPTABLE TO DO ANYTHING NECESSARY TO KILL THE MURDERER...

I'M A CHILD, BUT I'M A HALF-VAMPIRE.

DON'T YOU SEE? HE *USED* ME.

NO! THAT WOULD ONLY START A WAR!!

THIS IS HIS CITY, AND I'M JUST AN ASSISTANT. WHICH WOULD YOU CHOOSE?

OF COURSE HE WOULD DO IT.

NO! NO...

HE'S PROBABLY SENDING SIGNALS TO HIS VAMPIRE FRIENDS EVEN NOW.

HE IS NOT COMING HERE TO SAVE ME...

THIS IS ALL GOING ACCORDING TO HIS PLAN!

IF YOU KILL ME UNPRO-VOKED, HE CAN RETURN THE FAVOUR SAFELY!

YOU STILL DON'T GET IT.

HE'LL BE BACK AT ANY MOMENT WITH OTHERS!

I'D LEAVE IF I WERE YOU!

N-NO! WHY WOULD YOU DO THAT?!

THERE'S NOTHING TO STOP ME KILLING *SNAKEY!*

SO I CAN'T KILL YOU! BIG DEAL!

BYU (ZIP)

IT IS POSSIBLE... CREPSLEY *WOULD*...

(GIRI) (GRIT)

BUT HIS DEATH CRIES WILL BE MUSIC TO MY EARS!

YOU SAID IT YOURSELF— I CAN'T KILL YOU.

SNAKEY ISN'T IDEAL. I CAN'T EAT HIM, AND I'M HUNGRY, YES I AM.

I NEED SOMETHING TO CARVE!!

YOUNG MURLOUGH IS IN A KILLING MOOD!

NO GOOD, HALF-VAMPIRE!

THEN KILL ME! I'LL SWAP PLACES WITH EVRA!

NO! DON'T DO IT! YOU CAN'T!

...MY... MY GIRL-FRIEND...

I-I'LL GIVE YOU...

...

AND WHO COULD YOU GIVE ME, DARREN SHAN?

WHO?!

WAIT! LEAVE EVRA ALONE! I'LL GIVE YOU SOMEBODY EVEN BETTER!

OOH.♪

DARREN SHAN'S TASTY GIRL-FRIEND...

...I'LL GIVE YOU... DEBBIE.

IF YOU SPARE EVRA'S LIFE...

I WOULDN'T TAKE ANY CHANCES, IF I WERE YOU...

...WHAT WILL HAPPEN IF MR. CREPSLEY AND THE GENERALS KILL YOU BEFORE THEY DISCOVER I'M ALIVE?

EVEN IF YOU LET ME GO FREE...

...YOU'LL HAVE TO LEAVE THE CITY RIGHT AWAY.

WHETHER YOU LIKE IT OR NOT...

YOU'LL WANT TO FEED BEFORE LEAVING, YES?

THAT'S WHY DEBBIE WOULD BE BETTER THAN EVRA.

YOU'LL NEED TO GET OUT FOR AT LEAST TWO OR THREE NIGHTS, UNTIL THIS BLOWS OVER.

I'LL MAKE SURE OUR DEAL IS EXPLAINED.

LEAVE THIS PLACE?

AND YOU CAN'T MESS WITH US AFTER THIS...

BUT ONLY IF WE HAVE A DEAL. I'M TRADING DEBBIE FOR EVRA.

I CAN GET YOU IN AND OUT QUICKLY, WITHOUT ANYBODY KNOWING.

I CAN TAKE YOU TO DEBBIE RIGHT AWAY.

BUT I HOPE THAT I CAN TAKE YOUR WORD ON THIS.

OH, YOU'RE CLEVER, ALL RIGHT.

I HAVE NO POWER. YOU'RE IN CONTROL. I JUST WANT TO SAVE EVRA.

HOW COULD I POSSIBLY AFFORD TO PLAY A TRICK ON YOU IN THIS SITUATION?

WE'LL BOTH GO HOME TO THE CIRQUE DU FREAK, OKAY?

DON'T WORRY, EVRA. I WON'T BE THAT LONG.

VERY WELL, THEN.

WE HAVE A DEAL.

...A *HUMAN*.

YOU'RE MY BEST FRIEND, EVRA. DEBBIE'S JUST A HUMAN I HAD A CRUSH ON.

IT'S THE ONLY WAY.

I'D RATHER DIE THAN TRADE DEBBIE'S LIFE FOR MINE.

...AS IF SHE WAS JUST A...A...

HOW CAN YOU GIVE HER UP...

HOW CAN YOU DO IT?

...JUST AN "ANIMAL"...

...I WAS GOING TO SAY...

ACTU-ALLY...

A SAFE, SECRET WAY, TO KEEP US FROM BEING SPOTTED...

NOW LEAD THE WAY.

TO A VAMPIRE IT'S THE SAME THING...

PATAN
(THUMP)

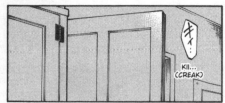

KII...
(CREAK)

YES
...

YOU CAN
SMELL IT
TOO, I BET,
HMMM?

YES,
YES!
I CAN
SMELL
HER
BLOOD
...

FUWA
(SLUF)

13

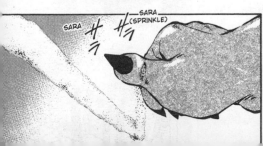

SARA
(SPRINKLE)

SARA

VAMPANEZE ALMOST NEVER KILL THEIR PREY IN ITS HOME. BUT WHEN WE HAVE TO...

...WE HAVE A RITUAL...

GUI (TUG)

I WANT YOU TO WATCH, DARREN SHAN.

WATCH AS I STEAL HER SOUL AND MAKE IT MINE...

I DO NOT LIKE TO FEED THIS WAY...

...BUT I HAVE NO CHOICE IN THE MATTER.

PARA (SPRINKLE)

GYU (SKRK)

IF YOU DON'T WATCH, I GO STRAIGHT TO THE PARENTS' ROOM AFTER THIS AND KILL THEM TOO.

THIS COULD BE THE MAKING OF YOU, BOY.

HEH-HEH... WHAT A GLARE.

YOU'RE A MON-STER!

NOTHING SOOTHES A HUNGRY STOMACH...

...LIKE THE RICH, SALTY SCENT...

GU (GRAB)

YOU MIGHT ENJOY IT MORE.

FANCY ABANDONING THAT BORING OLD VAMPIRE AND BECOMING YOUNG MURLOUGH'S ASSISTANT?

CHA (CHK)

CHA (CHK)

MMM...

HEH-HEH-HEH...

BA (RIP)

...OF BLOOD!!!

ZA (ZSH)

HI (CHEE) HI

ZAKU (ZLASH)

HMM?!

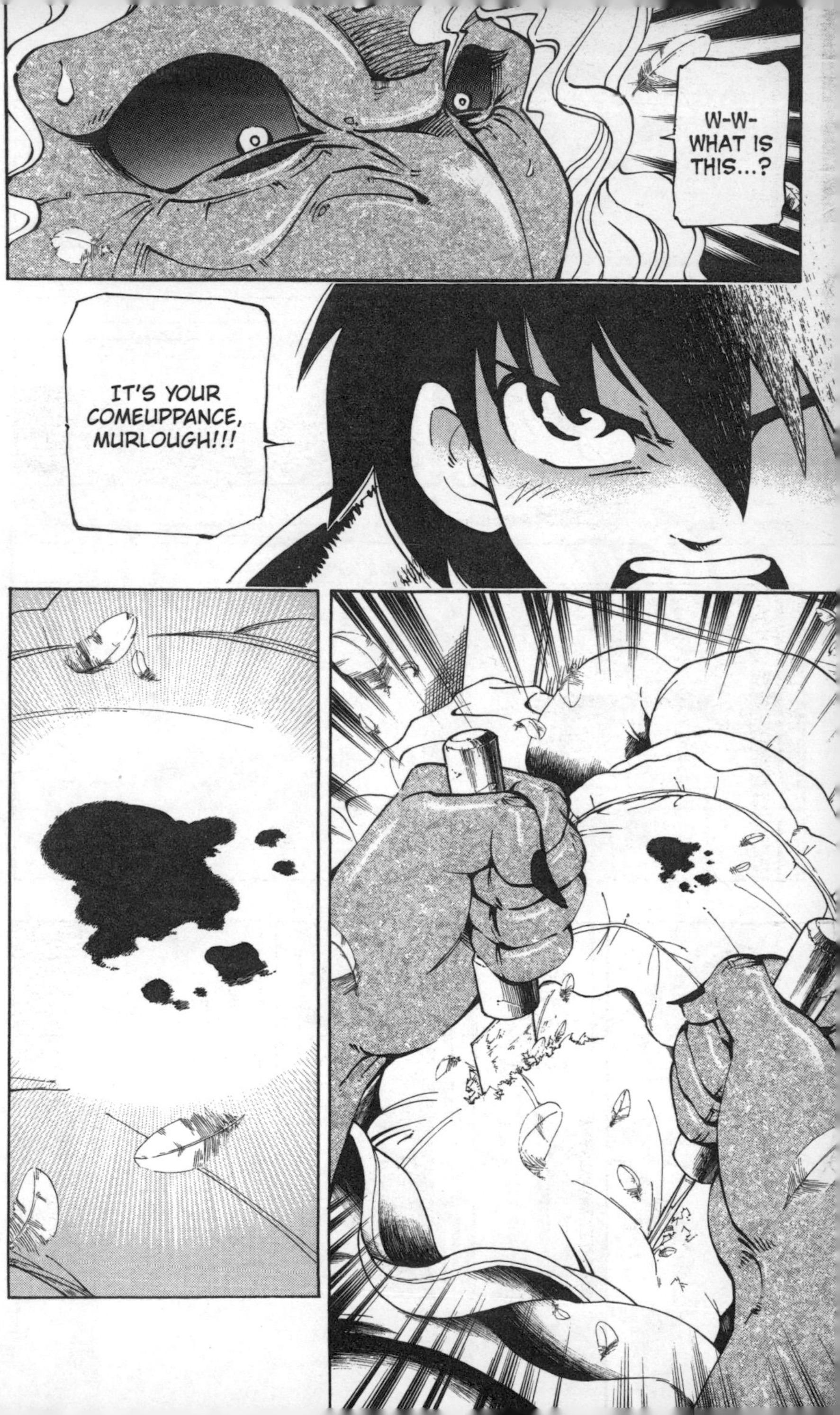
W-W-WHAT IS THIS...?
IT'S YOUR COMEUPPANCE, MURLOUGH!!!

SUUU
(ZZZ)

SUUU スーッ
スーッ
スーッ

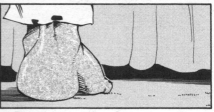

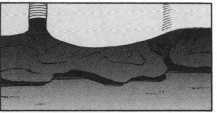

HOW CAN THIS BE...?

BUT... BUT...

MERRY CHRIST-MAS, MUR-LOUGH...

GIKII (CREAAAK)

THE DATE HAS JUST CHANGED.

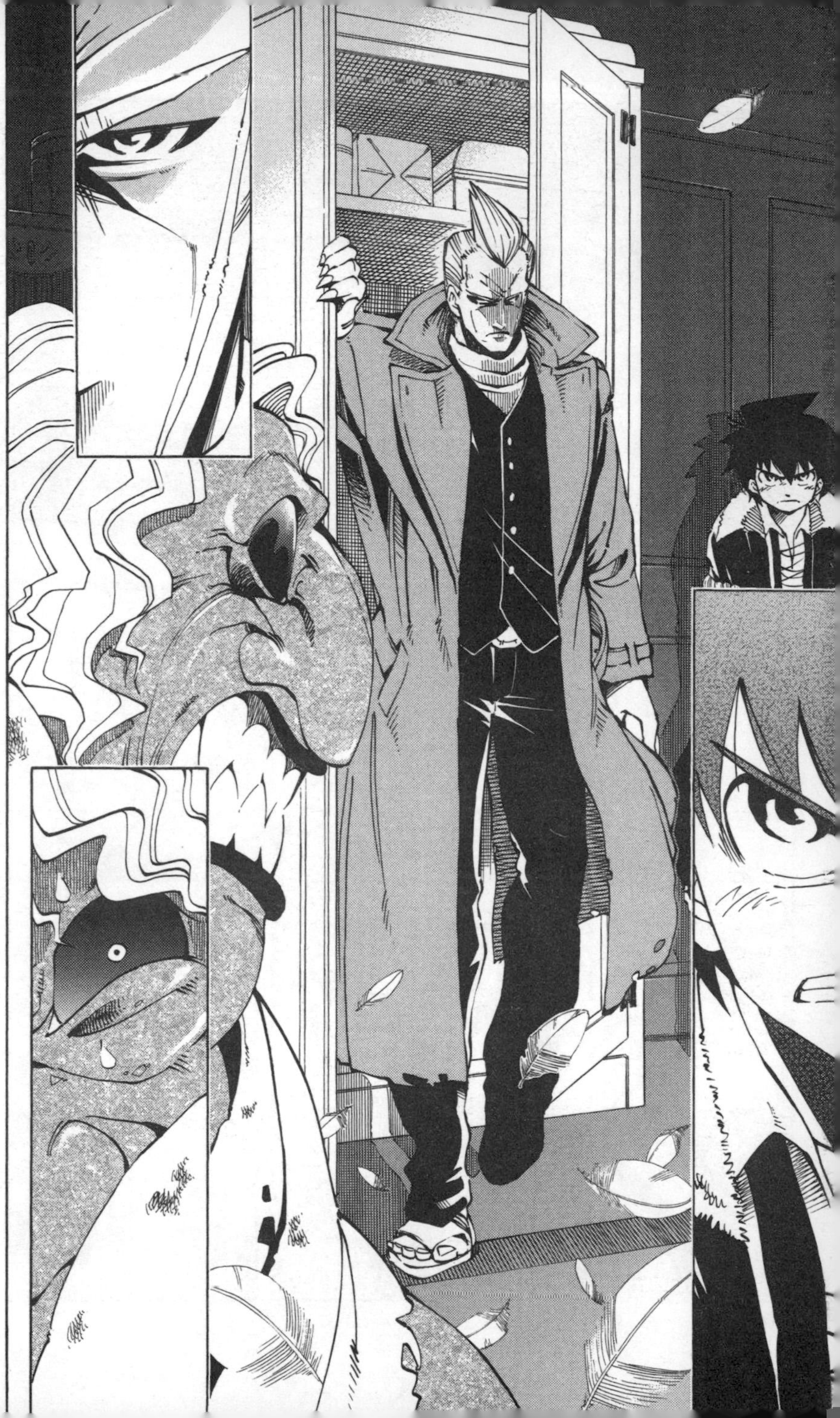

CHAPTER 24:
BATTLE TO THE DEATH

...AS A TENSE, CLOSE BATTLE PLAYED OUT OVER LONG MINUTES.

...CREATURES OF DARKNESS WOULD TRADE FOUL INSULTS...

IN THE MOVIES I'D SEEN...

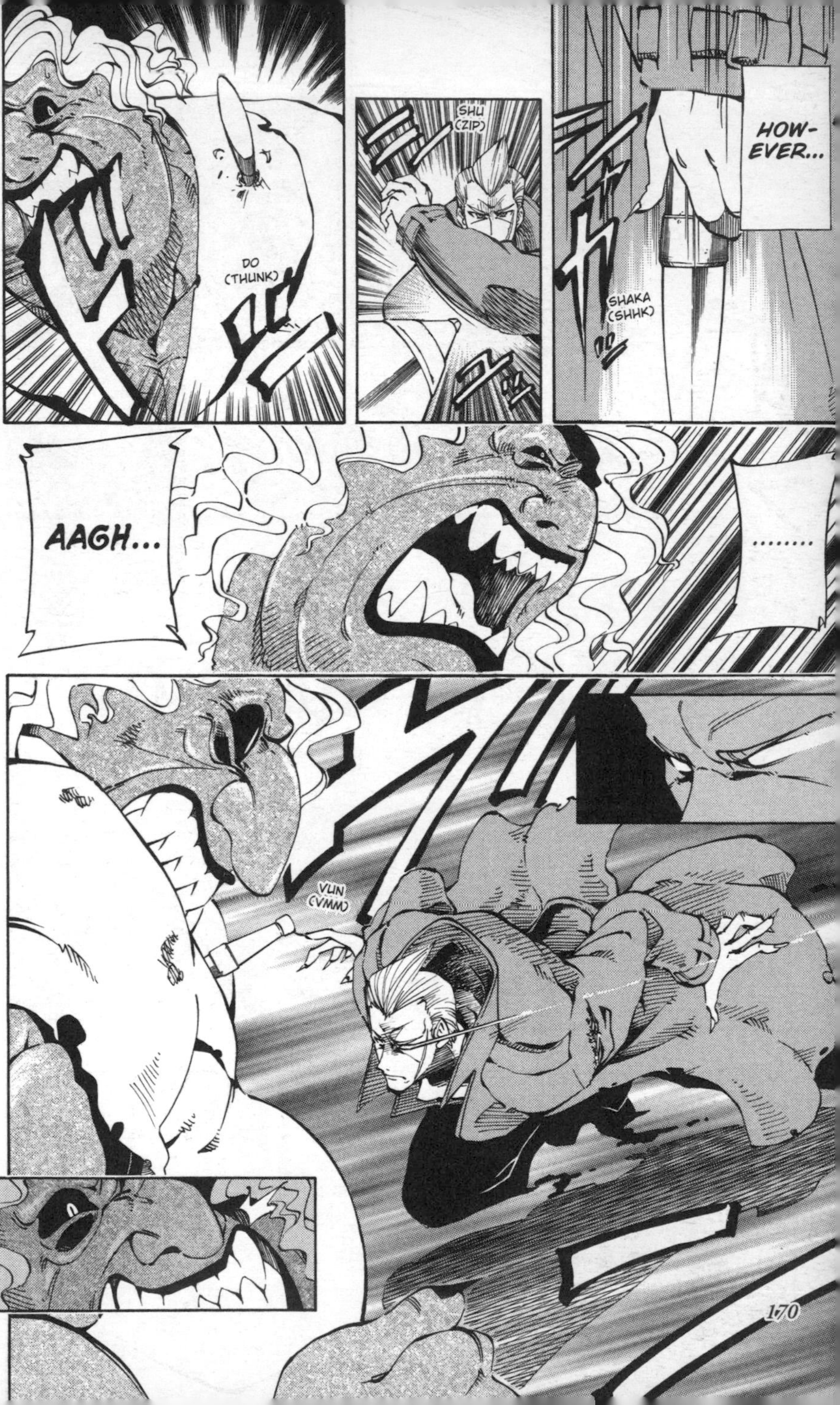
HOW-EVER...
SHAKA (SHHK)
SHU (ZIP)
DO (THUNK)
....
AAGH...
VUN (VMM)

ZUBA
(ZWOOSH)

BIHYU
(SWISH)

BOTATA
(DRIP
DRIP)

POTA
(DRIP)

...IN
REAL
LIFE,
IT WAS
DIFFER-
ENT.

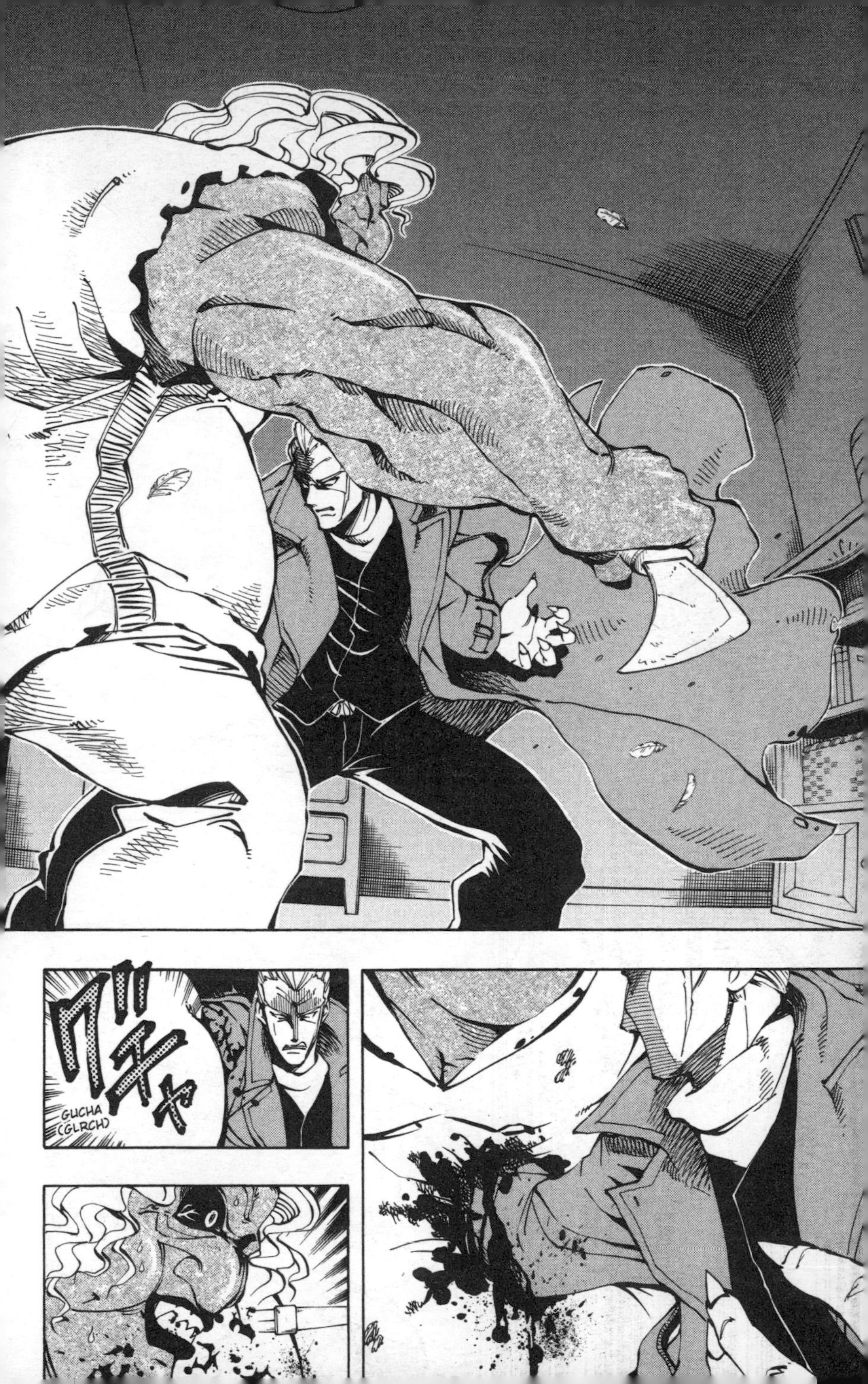
GUCHA
(GLRCH)

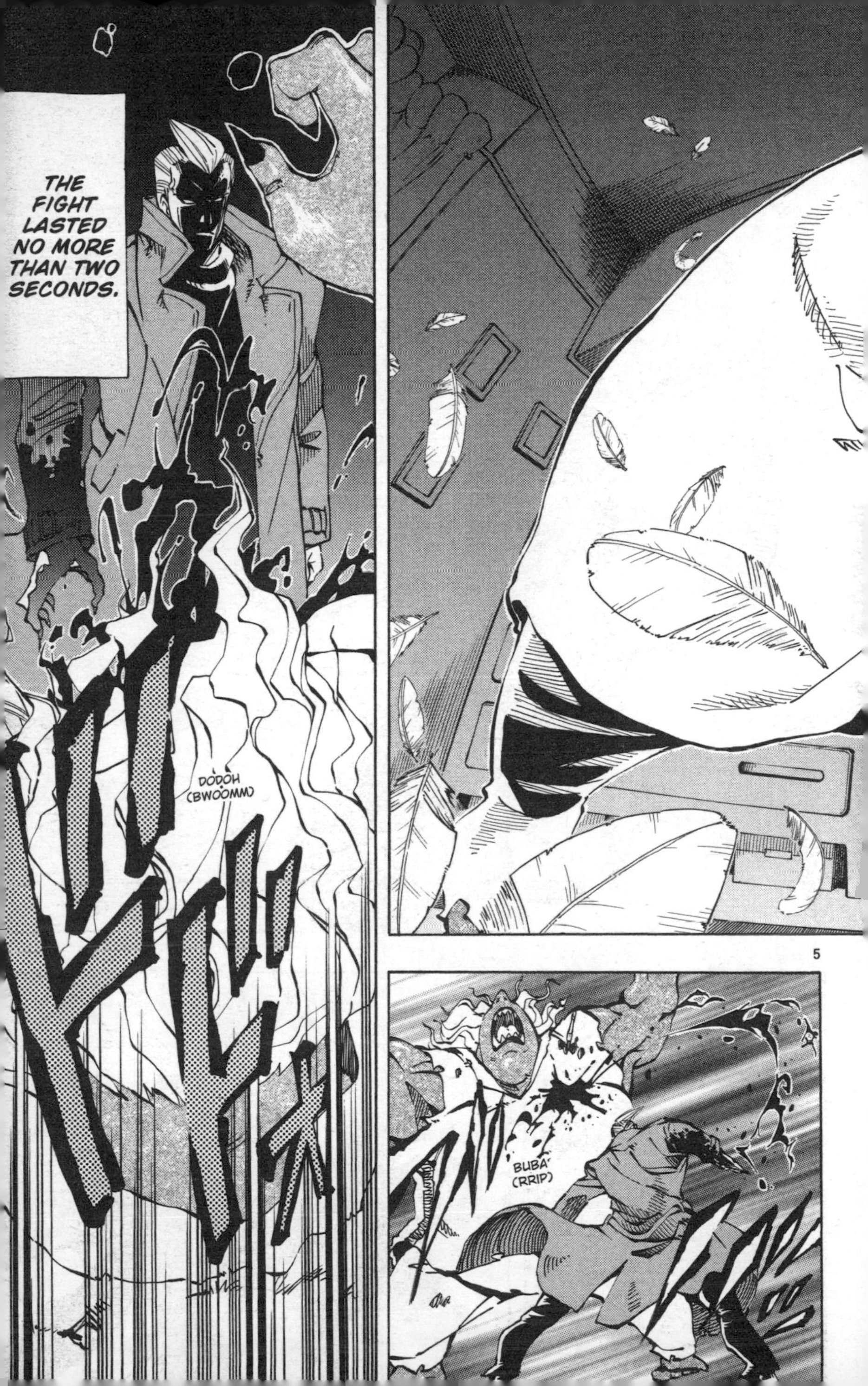
BUBA
(RRIP)
THE FIGHT LASTED NO MORE THAN TWO SECONDS.
DODOH
(BWOOMM)

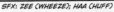

SFX: ZEE (WHEEZE); HAA (HUFF)

SFX: BECHA (SMEAR) BECHA

ZURU

ZURU
(DRAG)

HA
HA
...

HA
HA
HA
HA
...

SFX: PATA (FLOP)

GIRO
(GLARE)

GAHA (HACK)

GAHA!

ZURU (DRAG)
ZURU!

DON'T WORRY. HE IS HARMLESS NOW.

MR. CREPSLEY...

SFX: KUI (POIK) KUI

C-C-CLOSER...

GOBO! (BLAGH)

7

KOKU (NOD)

CLUH-
CLUH-
CLEVER
BUH-BUH-
BUH-BOY,
HMMM?

AND MUR-LOUGH WAS DEAD.

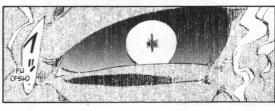

FU
(FSH)

MURLOUGH...

176

GAKU
(FLOP)

THE ENTIRE NIGHT HAD BEEN PLANNED OUT BY ME AND MR. CREPSLEY.

DEBBIE AND HER PARENTS WON'T BE AWAKE FOR SEVERAL HOURS YET.

I PUT SLEEP-ING POTION IN THE WINE.

I WENT AROUND THE BACK OF DEBBIE'S HOUSE TO MAKE SURE MURLOUGH DIDN'T SEE ME.

I HAD A "FIGHT" WITH MR. CREPSLEY, AND INTENTIONALLY GOT CAUGHT BY MURLOUGH.

WE HAD BEEN DEALING WITH A MAD VAMPANEZE, AND THERE WAS NO TELLING WHAT COULD HAVE GONE WRONG.

NUCHA (WIPE)

IT HADN'T BEEN A PERFECT PLAN.

IT WAS RISKING FIVE LIVES FOR THE SAKE OF ONE, AND IT WASN'T FAIR...

WE GOT THE HEMLOCKS INVOLVED IN A GAMBLE TO SAVE EVRA'S LIFE.

HE STILL MIGHT HAVE BEATEN MR. CREPSLEY IN THEIR BATTLE.

I STILL HAD TO CONVINCE HIM TO TAKE DEBBIE OVER EVRA.

I COULDN'T HAVE DONE IT WITH-OUT YOU... THANKS, SAM.

... BUT WE DIDN'T HAVE A CHOICE.

 SUU

SUU (ZZZ)

IT WAS NECESSARY TO MISLEAD MURLOUGH'S SENSE OF SMELL.

PASA (FLAP)

THERE'S THE MARK THAT CREPSLEY LEFT.

WE THEN PLACED HER UNDERNEATH THE BED.

HE DREW HER BLOOD TO PUT UNDER HER SHEETS.

I WAS *YOUR* PLAN. I SHOULD BE THE ONE OFFERING THANKS.

I DID WHAT HAD TO BE DONE.

ONLY BE-CAUSE OF SAM AND YOU.

THE PLAN WORKED BRILLIANTLY, DARREN.

HA-HA... THEN WE ARE EVEN.

IT WAS MY FAULT WE HAD TO RESORT TO THIS AT ALL...

THANK ME? NO...

WE SHALL BURY HIM IN THOSE UNDER-GROUND TUNNELS.

...BUT MURLOUGH WAS A LONE WOLF. I FEEL WE SHOULD BE SAFE.

THE VAMPANEZE WILL HUNT US TO THE ENDS OF THE EARTH IF THEY FIND THE BODY...

OKAY...

WE WILL FREE EVRA.

ONCE YOU ARE FINISHED HERE, COME DOWN TO FIND ME.

ZURU (DRAG)

ZURU

MURLOUGH *DID* LIKE THEM. HE'LL BE HAPPY DOWN THERE.

KOTO
(THUNK)
コト…

スー
ッ!
suuu
(ZZZ)

スー
ッ!
suuu

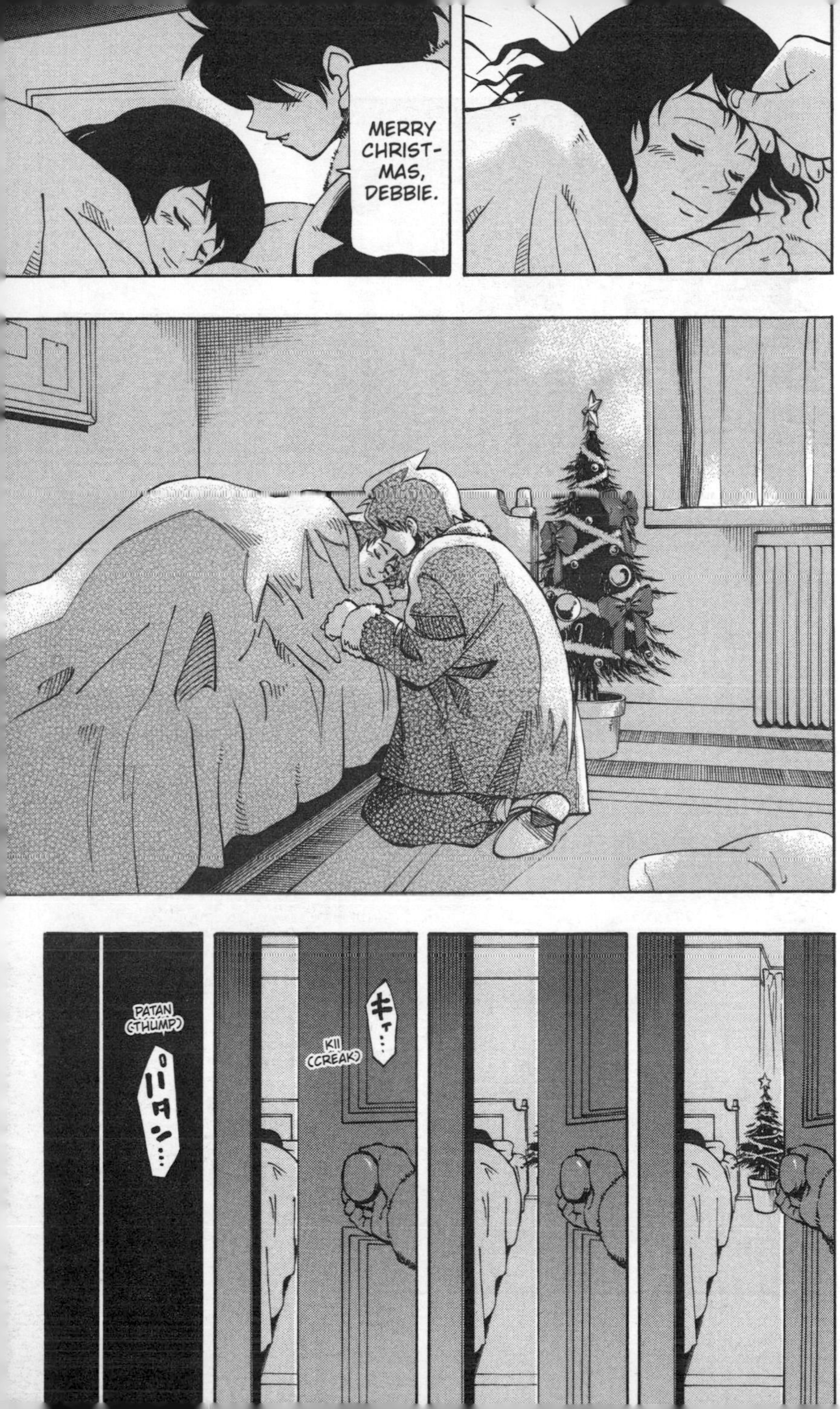

MERRY CHRIST-MAS, DEBBIE.
PATAN (THUMP)
パタン…
キィ…
KII (CREAK)

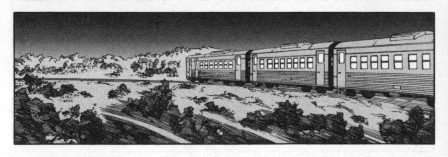

I'M SORRY, EVRA, I REALLY AM.

IT WASN'T RIGHT OF ME TO PUT YOU THROUGH THAT...

GOTON (TONK)

GATAN (TANK)

MUSL CHRMP

I THOUGHT YOU WERE CRAZY, OFFERING DEBBIE UP LIKE THAT!

YOU'RE DARN RIGHT, IT WASN'T!

BUT I THINK YOUR ANGER IS WHAT HELPED CONVINCE MURLOUGH I WAS TELLING THE TRUTH.

OH YEAH, I GUESS I'VE STILL GOT TIME!

GOSO GOSO (RUSTLE)

OPEN IT AND SEE!

WHAT IS THIS?

MERRY CHRISTMAS, EVRA!

OH!

BIRI

BIRI (RIP)

CHRIST-MAS ISN'T SO BAD, AFTER ALL...

HEH HEH...

YOU REALLY LIKED THAT BAND ON TV...

SURE!

...AND THANKS FOR THE PRES-ENT.

THANKS FOR SAVING ME, DARREN...

I'VE ALSO GOT ONE FOR YOU, MR. CREPSLEY...

MR. CREPS-LEY?

184

GOTON
GATAN

カタン
ゴトン

GOTON
GATAN

ガタン

カタン

(TANK)

GATAN
(TONK)

ガタ
ン

HA-HA-HA! THAT'S HILARIOUS, DARREN!

ズー！

AHA

HA

HA

HA

HA

HA

HA

SFX: ZUUN (CHMMM)

...

HMM? OH... WHAT IS THIS?

MERRY CHRIST-MAS, MR. CREPSLEY!

BIRI
(RIP)

ビリ

ビリ

BIRI

RIDICU-LOUS...

HMPH
...

REALLY?

I DON'T NEED ONE. I ALREADY GOT MY PRESENT.

I DON'T HAVE ANY-THING TO GIVE YOU!

DAMN!

THANKS, DEBBIE...

...AND GOODBYE.

TUNNELS OF BLOOD - END

A QUICK GUIDE TO THE STORY OF THE CIRQUE DU FREAK MANGA VERSION (SORT OF)!! PART 3!!!

RRGH!

THE BACKGROUNDS DEPICTING A FICTIONAL WORLD ARE THE BACKBONE OF ANY FANTASY MANGA.

MANGA BACKGROUNDS

THANKS FOR ALL THE HARD WORK, GUYS...

GATHERING REFERENCE MATERIALS IS A NECESSARY PART OF CREATING BACKGROUND ART.

WHEN IT'S DONE RIGHT, A BACKGROUND TURNS A FLAT PIECE OF PAPER INTO A THREE-DIMENSIONAL SPACE WITH REAL PRESENCE.

IT'S HUGE!

...BUT IN THE CASE OF THIS MANGA, I WAS ABLE TO GET GREAT USE OF THE PHOTOS I TOOK IN SCOTLAND WHEN I WAS LIVING THERE AS A BOY.

I RE-MEMBER THESE DAYS...

THERE ARE MANY WAYS TO GET MATERIALS, LIKE PHOTO BOOKS AND THE INTERNET...

PICHI ピチ

PICHI (WAG) ピチ

I SPENT MY VALUABLE TADPOLE DAYS THERE AS PART OF MY FATHER'S WORK.

ゴォォォ
GOHHH (WHOOOSH)

I SUPPOSE I MUST HAVE FORGOTTEN IT ALL WHEN I GREW MY LEGS.

OH MY!

SHOCKINGLY ENOUGH, I CAN BARELY SPEAK A WORD OF ENGLISH ANYMORE.

BOTH BROTHERS SUFFER AMNESIA...

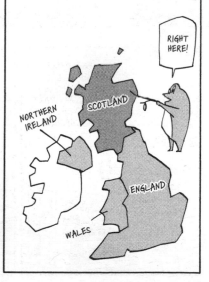

THE UNITED KINGDOM OF GREAT BRITAIN AND NORTHERN IRELAND!!

SCOTLAND IS ONE OF THE FOUR CONSTITUENT COUNTRIES THAT MAKE UP THE UNITED KINGDOM.

RIGHT HERE!

NORTHERN IRELAND

SCOTLAND

ENGLAND

WALES

200% GLAMORIZED

IT WASN'T THIS FANCY, THOUGH.

PICHI (WAG) PICHI

IN FACT, DARREN'S HOUSE BACK IN VOLUME 1 WAS BASED ON MY HOME IN SCOTLAND.

IT'S EASY TO SEE WHY MANY FAMOUS FANTASY STORIES, INCLUDING CIRQUE DU FREAK, COME FROM GREAT BRITAIN.

SEEING THE SIGHTS OF SCOTLAND IS LIKE DIVING INTO A FANTASY WORLD.

IF YOU HOPPED THE FENCE BEHIND THE HOUSE, YOU WERE IN A GOLF COURSE. I'D GET ALL SANDY PLAYING IN THE BUNKERS. (DON'T FOLLOW MY EXAMPLE, KIDS.)

HISSSS!!

BLACK, HARD, HEAVY, AND FAT...

AND THEIR SLUGS ARE MONSTER-SIZED!

ABOUT FOUR INCHES LONG!

GORO

GORO (ROLL)

ブ

ブロ...

ド (BOP)

THE SAND'S SO SILKY SMOOTH!

BIG BROTHER!

FOCUS YOUR EARS IN A FIELD AT NIGHT, AND YOU'LL HEAR SOME EERIE NOISES.

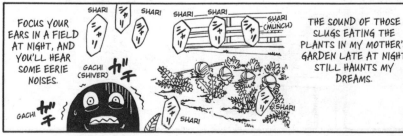

SHARI

シャリ

SHARI

SHARI

SHARI

SHARI (MUNCH)

GACHI (SHIVER)

ガチ

GACHI

ガチ

SHARI

シャリ

SHARI

THE SOUND OF THOSE SLUGS EATING THE PLANTS IN MY MOTHER'S GARDEN LATE AT NIGHT STILL HAUNTS MY DREAMS.

MY FRIENDS AND I BUILDING A SECRET TREE FORT WITH SCRAP WOOD FROM A NEARBY TIMBER YARD...

...IS A DEAR MEMORY I STILL TREASURE.

LITTLE BRO'S TOO SMALL TO HELP OUT.

IN THE SUMMERTIME, IT'S STILL BRIGHT OUT UNTIL NINE IN THE EVENING, SO YOU CAN ACTUALLY SPEND THE ENTIRE DAY PLAYING OUTSIDE.

WAA (RAHH)

WAA

FRISBEE!

THEY WERE A GREAT SOURCE OF STRENGTH WHEN I HAD JUST STARTED THE MANGA AND HAD VERY LITTLE REFERENCE MATERIAL TO WORK WITH.

THE PHOTOS WE HAD OF SCOTTISH TOWNS AS A KID REALLY HELPED OUT WITH MAKING VOLUME 3.

IF I HAD THE TIME AND MONEY, I'D LOVE TO VISIT SCOTLAND AGAIN. IT'S A GORGEOUS PLACE.

POKEEE (DAAAZE)

THE SETTING SUN IS BEAUTIFUL FROM THE BALCONY OF MY WORKPLACE.

I REALLY OWE MY PARENTS FOR TAKING ALL OF THOSE PICTURES AND KEEPING THEM.

The End

THE SAGA OF DARREN SHAN ③
Tunnels of Blood

Darren Shan
Takahiro Arai

Translation: Stephen Paul
Lettering: AndWorld Design
Original cover design: Hitoshi SHIRAYAMA + Bay Bridge Studio

Darren Shan Vol. 3
Text © 2007 Darren Shan, Artworks © 2007 Takahiro ARAI
All rights reserved
Original Japanese edition published in Japan in 2007
by Shogakukan Inc., Tokyo
Artwork reproduction rights in U.K. and The Commonwealth arranged
with Shogakukan Inc. through Tuttle-Mori Agency, Inc., Tokyo.

English translations © Darren Shan 2009

Published in Great Britain by Harper Collins *Children's Books* 2009
Harper Collins *Children's Books* is a division of HarperCollins *Publishers* Ltd
77-85 Fulham Palace Road, Hammersmith, London, W6 8JB

www.harpercollins.co.uk

2

ISBN: 978 0 00 732089 9

Printed and bound in Great Britain by Clays Ltd, St Ives plc

Mixed Sources
Product group from well-managed
forests and other controlled sources
www.fsc.org Cert no. SW-COC-1806
© 1996 Forest Stewardship Council
FSC

FSC is a non-profit international organisation established to promote the
responsible management of the world's forests. Products carrying the FSC
label are independently certified to assure consumers that they come
from forests that are managed to meet the social, economic and
ecological needs of present and future generations.

Find out more about HarperCollins and the environment at
www.harpercollins.co.uk/green